Vasanth Kannabiran is a veteran civil and women's rights activist, and a well-known teacher, writer and translator. Her published works include, *My Life is a Song: Gaddar's Anthems for the Revolution* (2021); *Softly Dies a Lake* (2020); a translation of Akkineni Kutumbarao's autobiographical novel, *Kolleti Jadalu*; *Taken at the Flood: A Memoir of a Political Life* (2019); and *A Grief to Bury: Memories of Love, Work and Loss* (2011). She has also written and produced the ballets, *Menaka*, *Ahalya*, *Gandhari* and *Rajasimha*, which have been performed in several cities.

Pankaja

VASANTH
KANNABIRAN

SPEAKING
TIGER

SPEAKING TIGER BOOKS LLP
125A, Ground Floor, Shahpur Jat, near Asiad Village,
New Delhi 110049

First published by Speaking Tiger Books 2022

ISBN: 978-93-5447-392-0
eISBN: 978-93-5447-393-7

10 9 8 7 6 5 4 3 2 1

Typeset in Dante MT Std by SÜRYA, New Delhi

Printed at Shree Maitrey Printech Pvt. Ltd., Noida

In earnest gratitude to my firstborn: Chitra Kannabiran,
Brilliant, incredibly wise and patient
Who taught me to weave disparate episodes into a story
Whose loving care preserves my sanity and health
In my twilight years.

Author's Note

This novel has been haunting me for many years. I began an attempt to pen it down nearly twenty years ago and then life took over and I laid it aside. All the tales here were told to me by grandmothers and aunts. Some I had witnessed. Gradually, as I finished the tasks that I had set myself, I found these stories, which had been thrust into some remote back chamber of my mind returning to haunt me.

I realised there was a pattern that weaved these seemingly stray anecdotes together; an invisible one of violence that held my grandmothers and great aunts in a delicate but ruthless web. This pattern that emerged from these disconnected anecdotes provides a rich picture of what it meant to be an upper-caste woman in the early twentieth century. I felt it was worth recording as it reflects the social history of certain sections at that moment of time.

Marriage, separation and loss are themes that have haunted me for many years. *A Grief to Bury* (OBS.2011), a collection of experiences revolving around marriage, the loss of partners and widowhood still remains my most significant work. However, as I went back to these remembered tales, mostly told with a touch of humour or a sprinkling of disgust, I came to realise that many of the cherished truths of that generation were mere fictions. Marriage, though mandatory, seldom guaranteed security or happiness. If one picked up random tales and threaded them together, new patterns emerged.

Widowhood and caste were critical markers of that era. While caste still rears its head in uglier and increasingly violent ways today, perceptions of both marriage and widowhood have changed radically. Yet, grief, betrayal and illusory perceptions of connubial bliss keep on haunting us.

What I share here with my readers is but a mere string of old wives' tales. There is no philosophy or moral intended to be drawn here. If inevitably some of my feminist philosophy has trickled in, the reader can safely ignore it. It is but a tale told by an idiot full of sound and fury. A clutch of whispered stories I heard as a child and relegated to some remote corner of my mind. Jokes whispered in undertones; throwaway references, chuckles, sighs and juicy gossip, which made no sense to my innocent ears. It was as I grew older that these old wives' tales became more strident, demanding my full attention.

When I reflected on the stories of the past, I saw a pattern emerging. The pattern of women's lived realities revealed the subtext of the dominant narrative, which spoke of conjugal bliss, wifely duty and the unparalleled power of chastity. As I remembered one story after another, they began to reveal a panorama of insights about marriage, sexuality, modernity and mythology.

This novel wrote itself. I only provided the ink. And I remain humbled by the wives, widows and whores in this tale who forced me to write it.

1

Relaxing in her easy chair in the front yard, Pankaja gazed at the pattern that the morning sun filtering in through the neem leaves cast at her feet. A few ripe neem fruits were scattered on the ground. Pigeons cooed from high above. Suddenly, a solitary crow cawed, shattering the peace of the moment. She wondered if a visitor would come. But the days when a cawing crow heralded the arrival of a guest were long gone. The world had changed so much.

She stared at a neem fruit, bitter and yet healing. The neem tree with its serrated leaves and rough bark reminded her of her own life. Her journey had been marked by joy, grief, trust, betrayal, triumph and tragedy. What was left was only bitterness, but this too was a feeling one could savour. She had learned to relish the neem—healing old wounds, freshening foul air and heralding with its delicate blooms a new year and new beginnings. She smiled at her own foolish hope. What new beginnings could she expect now save a painless and dignified end? For she had seen it all. And foreseen it all…

Smiling, she dozed off in the warmth of the morning sun.

2

The lamp flickered in the dark room. Lying on a worn mat on the floor, Pattamma heaved and groaned. Clenching her teeth to prevent herself from screaming, she pushed, as the contractions came one after the other in quick succession. The midwife held her head and said, 'Push a little harder, it's almost here.' Turning to the mother who was cringing in the dark, she muttered, 'What misfortune for this cursed girl. Like a golden image. Her first born and she is a widow! It's all Bhagvan's *maya*. The fruit of her sins in the last life. *Aiyyo*, Rama!'

Pattamma screamed and pushed and the child's head emerged. The midwife held the head and with one more push, the baby slipped into her hands. A beautiful boy. Big and fair. Snipping and binding his umbilical cord, she cooed and set him down on an old mat spread on the floor before attending to Pattamma.

Pressing out the afterbirth, she wrapped it in a banana leaf and placed it in a corner.

She washed the child in lukewarm water, wrapped him in an old cloth and handed him to his grandmother. Muttering to herself, she started clearing the room in the dim light. 'A first-born boy! If that mother hadn't been a wretched widow, she would have got a handsome gift.' Rajamma looked at the baby sadly, sighed and handed him to his mother.

Pattamma turned her face away and looked at the wall in the dimly-lit room. Stained and cracked, the wall was just like her life. Gazing at the child's face, her dead husband's face floated before her eyes. Middle-aged, paralysed from the waist downwards, he had suffered a heart attack when he heard his wife was pregnant. He had simply died of shame.

Pattamma's father had fixed this match to an elderly wealthy man, thinking that if she bore him just one child, his beautiful daughter's life would be secure. She would be spared the poverty and hunger that had dogged their lives all along. The acre of land they had was barely enough to survive on. But fate was cruel and the elderly son-in-law suffered a stroke. His large house in PR Square was filled with relatives and friends who flocked to visit him. They eyed the beautiful young bride, and sympathised with his plight.

Gradually, he grew worse and became completely bedridden. The spark of desire he had felt for his child-bride and the faint hope that her fresh, young blood would revive his worn-out body, remained unfulfilled. In spite of his anxiety about her safety, he could do little to protect her from the vultures who circled his home. He would try to speak to her but his speech was slurred. At times, he grunted painfully, struggling to raise his hand and hold her. But both words and actions had been torn away from him by a cruel stroke of fate.

Pattamma waited on him cheerfully and patiently, never displaying any revulsion or hesitation at his pitiful condition. But barely fourteen, when his friends brushed up against her or looked at her with their heavy-lidded eyes, she was confused and aroused. This was a strange feeling. Her young body yearned for something. She sensed that this yearning was not a good thing, but she did not dare confide in her mother.

Soon, Rajamma left for Pondavakkam to attend to her field, leaving the coast clear for his friends to make their moves. And inevitably, one day, after having been pushed into a corner and handled roughly, but strangely excitingly, by one of his friends, Pattamma discovered a sheltered corner of the large house where her newly roused desires and yearning flesh could be satisfied by these hungry men. The problem, however, was managing them. Though young, she was proud and quick, and chose her lovers with care. They saw to it that she was safe from other predators.

There was one lawyer in particular, called Varadan (nickname: Papa), who was a self-appointed guardian of her virtue. When she was pregnant, he assumed that it was his child little knowing that there were at least three other men who could make the same assumption. To give the devil his due, Papa managed the whole tragedy of her husband's heart attack with tact and discretion, not allowing a whisper of accusation or gossip to touch Pattamma.

Her husband's funeral rites and ceremonies were conducted quietly, leaving Pattamma in peace. Her pregnancy protected her from much of the shame that marked a widow. Soon after forty days were over, Papa made arrangements for her to go back to her mother's home in Pondavakkam, accompanied by her mother and aunt.

3

Pondavakkam was a homely village with houses clustered around a Vishnu temple. Originally a settlement of about thirty Brahmin families who tended the Vishnu temple, it soon attracted other castes, who occupied it, finding the land fertile and the water clean. And because other castes had crept in too, the village was known as Pondavakkam—the place occupied by migrants. Rajamma's family being one of the first to settle there, commanded a measure of respect. The women left the house of misfortune in Madras with a sigh of relief. Reaching home, they felt sheltered and safe. Nothing could harm them here.

Rajamma was in the backyard, drawing water from a well. Pouring the water into a brass pot, she peered at the creeper crawling along the wall to see if the pumpkin was ready to be plucked. Parting the furry leaves, she gazed at the pumpkin. She could leave it for another day or two and cook the *kovakkai* (small gourd) that was growing in profusion. It was sure to increase Pattama's breast milk. The child was healthy, growing rapidly and always hungry. She felt he was sucking all his mother's strength out. And he was too young to be weaned.

Perhaps next month, she could try some of the black-and-white cow's milk. The cow was yielding profusely. The farmer who was cultivating their paddy field had not yet brought the bags of rice and husked tamarind that were due this month. She must send Vasu, who lived next door, to remind him before he sold off some of it. He was a good man but times were hard.

'Remember, Rajamma! You have a pumpkin growing inside a fragile pot. You have a heavy responsibility. You must protect the pumpkin and let it grow fully and take care to see that the pot doesn't crack,' her sister, Chinnamma, warned.

On hearing that Pattamma had delivered a son, Varadan promptly set off to Pondavakkam. Alighting at the bus station, he packed a bullock cart with baskets of fruits, flowers, coconuts and sweets that he had brought in the pride of his presumed fatherhood. Covering her mouth with her *pallu* (sari's end), Pattamma rushed to the front door to welcome him. There he was, smiling and bustling with self-importance, standing at her door. At his feet were baskets laden with flowers, fruits and sweets. The neighbours' eyes widened as their hands went up to cover their mouths at this gross spectacle. Such luxurious gifts for a miserable widow's birthing! Govinda!

Rajamma managed to usher him into the house deftly. After saying a few firm words, she let him gaze at Pattamma and the child for a moment. Serving him a tumbler of hot coffee, she asked him to leave quickly before the whole village gathered to stare. Pattamma was amused but neither flattered nor flustered by his arrival. Looking at the gifts he had brought, she smiled, then turned away. His anxious pleas about her health were met with a smile and a shrug of her shapely bare shoulders. In the end, it was the respect Rajamma commanded and the neighbours' sympathy for her condition that saved the day from turning into a disaster.

Amma Rajamma by all standards was a rare beauty. She wore only a diamond nose ring as a symbol of her wifely status, a pair of plain earrings and a yellow thread with a *taali* (wedding necklace) around her neck. The rest of the jewellery had been sold over the years to keep the family going. But her finely chiselled features and stark simplicity only served to underline her dignity and noble bearing. Her daughters were also breathtakingly beautiful just like her. Pattamma, a statuesque beauty with a regal bearing and Pankaja, a curly-haired, bright-eyed, dimpled beauty with black curls that refused to be cowed down by a plait.

People often referred to their home as a house with three silver *kuthu vilakkus* (tall lamps with five wicks), which blazed bright day and night. But as God wills, most blessings tend to be short lived. And the evil eye she feared even more than hunger or poverty soon snuffed out that brightness. First, her own flame was extinguished. Krishnan, her husband who suffered from excruciating pain in the stomach, which could be calmed only with a smear of opium, grew worse.

He had to be tied to the wooden pillar in front of the house to be controlled. And he screamed day and night in pain, pleading for relief. She sold everything she could to keep him calm. The silver plates, the brass pots, her jewellery: one by one, all gone. But it was not enough. Nothing was ever enough to keep him quiet and ease the demon that plagued him. She suffered for him but she still had to think of Pankaja's future. So, in one way, his death was a respite when it came. She did not shave her head or wear white; though she went through the other rituals.

Unfortunately, misfortunes never come singly. Following close on her heels, her daughter Pattamma was widowed. Within a year of her husband's death, her son-in-law passed away. Rajan was a wealthy but elderly man who was childless. He had lost his wife a few years ago. Her husband had fixed this match against Pattamma's wishes.

'Our beautiful daughter! That priceless pearl! How can you even think of this? She is sure to get a good match. Do not be hasty and throw away her future,' she had pleaded with her senseless husband.

'Let her just bear a son; one son and her future is secure forever. Just look at all that property. How long does youth last anyway?' he had asked.

Her son-in-law's death shook Rajamma to the core. Now, the house which had sparkled with the beauty of her daughters and her quiet dignity, the splendid house of three *kuthu vilakkus*, had turned into the miserable abode of three widows. The third widow was her sister Chinnamma, who had come to live with them after her husband died of typhoid. However, unlike most other widows of their time, miserable, victimised and ill-treated, the three women were quite independent, efficient and capable of managing the little land they had. They had the will to survive despite their misfortunes.

But the stigma of widowhood remained. All said and done a widow is a widow and society considers her a symbol of misfortune. The contempt it evoked stung Rajamma bitterly and shamed her deeply. But with two daughters, one widowed and the other yet to be married, she could ill afford the luxury of grief or shame. She had to garner her strength and protect her family. She had brought Pattamma back home soon after the funeral rites were over.

Young Pattamma did not seem greatly shattered by the tragedy. She shed a few bitter tears when the women started keening around her, but truth be told it was more the sound of their weeping than the fact of her husband's death that disturbed her. After all, she had barely known her husband. And these labels mattered little to her. But there was a child growing inside her. A widow's child. She hunkered down and decided that she would never let her offspring suffer a tainted existence. Her child had to be protected at all costs.

Closing her eyes, she shut out the sight of the wailing women.

'What ill fortune! What a miserable fate! Look at all that beautiful hair. *Aiyyo*! All of it destined for the barber's knife. Who can bear to look upon that face then? Wretched girl. How can you escape the sins of your previous *janma* (birth)? Govinda!'

These words hardened Pattamma's young heart. She would not let them disfigure her. Not for this mockery of a marriage and this shadow of a husband. She told her mother that if anyone attempted to lay their hands on her, she would run away. She would find one of those hostels for young widows that Sister Subbalakshmi had set up or else just walk straight into the sea. But submit to such indignity she would not!

Rajamma turned around to face the criticism. She fiercely shielded her daughter and refused to let them lay their hands on her. And Pattamma was spared. Her good fortune was that there were no men in the family. No stern self-righteous father or uncle committed to uphold custom at the expense of the women. With a dead father and a brother who had vanished as a boy, theirs was a family of women. In the midst of all the despair, there was still a ray of hope for the women, nourished by their steadfast love for each other and the confidence that they could survive in the village.

4

Pattamma was literate and well read. In spite of her minimal schooling, she was drawn to the treasures that letters seemed to hold. She greedily devoured papers or books that came her way and encouraged Pankaja to read too. She kept a notebook and wrote down little notes. She liked to read the news. She even read the newspaper wrappings in which provisions were sold. She read about the freedom struggle, satyagraha, the youth and the women pouring into the streets braving *lathis* (kicks) and bullets to fight for freedom and women stripping off their jewels and handing them over to Gandhiji. She read Gandhiji's speeches and listened to the radio, which was her lifeline. She also followed all the other Congress leaders eagerly.

She was curious and intelligent. For a poor, young Brahmin widow from a backward village, her interest in and knowledge of the huge upheavals in the country were vast. Rajaji was a leader she admired with all her heart. She was deeply moved by his appeal to wear *khaddar* and save the virtue of the women whose husbands had been shipped off by the British as indentured labour. Left behind with small children, their only means of survival was prostitution. She wondered whether spinning yarn could fill their bellies.

But Rajaji had sent out a sincere appeal. He must know. And in the middle of all these major upheavals, she had a young son to bring up. It did not take much effort though. Rajappa was a golden child and she had her aunt and sister to help her. He thrived in the warmth and the care of these women. One of them, Pankaja, was still a slip of a girl.

Soon, twenty-one days had passed, the child was laid on a bed of paddy that was spread on the ground, and Pattamma traced his name in the paddy with her forefinger. He was named Srinivasa Raghavan and handed over to his mother. Pattamma, wearing a clean old silk without any blouse or jewellery, seemed calm and composed as she laid her lips against his tiny ear and whispered his name thrice. What would have been a grand festival if the father was alive was a quiet, modest ceremony.

When the old aunt in the corner began to keen in grief, Pattamma clicked her tongue sharply and the sound stopped. The few neighbours who were taking their *kumkum* (a red pigment used by Hindu women to make a round mark on the forehead) and betel leaves and coconuts from the second daughter, Pankaja, sighed heavily and murmuring a blessing, left. A few of them pressed a rupee coin each into the baby's tiny palm.

Pankaja was the only one in that household untainted by widowhood and worthy of offering the ritual betel leaves, nuts and coconuts to the *sumangalis* (married women) who were thought to bring blessings of good fortune and wealth. A married woman with turmeric and *kumkum* was considered the incarnation of Lakshmi herself. The family was together again and looked at the baby in delight.

He was a golden child, strong-limbed and lusty, bringing a golden ray of hope into their darkest despair. Rajamma crooned a lullaby to him, rocking his hammock made out of an old silk sari. Her bruised heart seemed to grow calm as the child gurgled pleasantly, listening to her sing.

Soon after the cradling ceremony, the village priest turned up and declared that since the purification and cradling ceremony were done, the widowhood rites were now due. It was time to shave Pattamma's head and give her, her widow's weeds. This had been delayed for so long only because she was carrying a child. Pattamma, barely fifteen, looked at him contemptuously. Her delicate nostrils, unburdened by diamonds, flared. She declared that there would be no further rites. She had cast off her *taali*, her jewellery and her blouse, and now not even Yama could come down to earth and force her to do anything more. The priest, who was taken aback by her fury, stammered and retreated. Rajamma, shaken by this attempt to disfigure her daughter again, was relieved that she had stood up to the priest.

5

They managed life reasonably well with the widowed aunt helping them out. A couple of years passed. It was time for Pankaja to settle down now. Rajamma fixed her marriage to a young man from a landed family in Nellore. Her cousin who lived in Nellore had suggested the match. She mortgaged the land to raise a loan for a simple wedding. And that duty of hers was done.

Fortunately for her, the family had not demanded any dowry. Just a decent wedding and the customary jewellery for the bride: compulsory diamonds for the earrings and nose pins; four pairs of gold bangles; a gold ring for the groom and the customary silverware. Then there were the silver plates and glasses for the bride and groom and a set of silver lamps, bells and a silver pot meant for puja. Many of these were salvaged from her own things.

She took care not to touch any of Pattamma's

articles. Partly because she might need them later, but also perhaps because she feared they were tainted by misfortune. On the whole, Rajamma managed to put together an adequate display. The groom's family was decent, not avaricious. They liked the girl and respected Rajamma whose dignity and status in her caste had remained untouched by poverty and misfortune.

Gopalan was studying medicine. The eldest son of the family, he was bronzed and neatly built. His sharp features, twinkling eyes and deep dimple added to his attractions. Quick-tempered and witty, he was adored by his sisters and his cousins. Soon, she came of age and it was time for Pankaja to leave for her father-in-law's house. Her young, handsome husband, Gopalan, arrived to pick up the mother and daughter and take them to Nellore. Though Rajamma had provided all the necessary gifts and offerings customary to a nuptial, she dared not visit the groom's house as she had not yet completed five years of widowhood. She was still considered tainted by misfortune.

She stayed in a *choultry* (hall) near the temple and saw her daughter off. Her pleas and prayers during those few days were countless. Every time she bathed in the Pennar, she wished the swirling waters would end her sorrow. But then she could not afford that luxury because she had another daughter to protect.

On the third day after the consummation, her son-in-law came to meet her and put her on a train that would take her back home. He did not think it necessary to bring young Pankaja along to say goodbye to her mother. Rajamma's heart yearned for a glimpse of her beloved child. Was she happy? Was she scared? Whose advice could she seek if frightened or confused in her husband's house? Well, God was there after all to take care of her.

Steadying her tremulous heart, she got on the train and huddled on a seat next to the window. Her son-in-law smiled, gave her a bunch of bananas and a pot of buttermilk, and wished her a safe journey. He left before the train took off. He had to get back to work. He was youthful and strong and that comforted her. He also owned a large house in the town as well as twenty acres of wet land in a nearby village. Pankaja would be happy with him by her side.

Rajamma, who could ill-afford to indulge her feelings, found grief choking her. She earnestly prayed that this young, healthy son-in-law of hers who was soon to be a doctor would ensure Pankaja's happiness. After all the suffering the child had seen...An ailing father. Soon, a mother widowed, followed by a widowed sister. She deserved to be happy and have a faithful, caring husband. The engine whistled, startling her out of her thoughts. As the train sped along, she sat all by herself, lost in thought. Soon, the train chugged into Madras Central. Picking up her bundle, she got off and found her way back to Pattamma's home.

Pankaja was calm and collected unlike her imperious sister. She swallowed her fear and grief at leaving her mother, and dutifully stood by her husband. He grasped her hand firmly and drew her close. His touch was comforting and her nervousness melted away. Pankaja was beautiful. Different from her sister whose statuesque beauty seemed carved of marble. She had thick black curls, which escaped the knot and framed her face. Her sisters-in-law teased her, saying she had a bob cut. Golden-skinned, slim-waisted and high-breasted, she was the very image of Goddess Meenakshi. And when the marriage was consummated, she was content. Her husband knew how to arouse and satisfy her. Life was good.

He could never have enough of her. He dimpled at her, called her 'madam' playfully, and snatched at her, pinching her waist when they stood behind the old pillars in their home. She was content, though often exhausted by his demands. He was young, hot-blooded and besotted with her. Her mother-in-law and sisters-in-law were relieved because he was quick-tempered by nature and difficult to manage. Pankaja seemed to wrap him around her little finger. They were made for each other; a perfect couple like Lakshmi and Vishnu. A joy to behold when they stood together. And the old couple was proud of them.

Her mother-in-law often worried that her son harassed Pankaja even when she was in the advanced stages of her pregnancy. Since he had insisted that she was to have her delivery in Nellore, where there was a Mission Hospital, he was by her side and hence, there was no period of enforced abstinence. If she had gone to her mother's home, she could have escaped his demands. When she whispered, 'don't', he grabbed her, saying, 'I am a doctor. You think I don't know what I am doing?'

He could never have enough of her. He was, however, gentle and passionate and she grew to enjoy him. But his lust could never be satisfied. When it was not possible to turn to her, he approached other women who gave in gladly. There was a lean, muscular Yenadhi woman, who cleaned the hospital yard and he often grabbed her to satisfy his lust. Though he was a good doctor, he had quite a reputation. Pankaja was not unduly disturbed by this. As her mother-in-law often said, 'A man will be a man!' He was affectionate. And proud of her beauty and intelligence. Why bother about these trivial flings? At night, he would always return to her bed after all. Of this, she was sure.

6

Pankaja stirred in her sleep. She remembered how she had longed to see her mother off. To say she was well. To lay her head on that comforting shoulder one last time. But she knew that asking for this could trigger a tirade from her sisters-in-law and her mother-in-law. Even her husband may be irritated. She had begun to learn the most important lesson to survive.

'Do not ask! Never ask! And you will not be humiliated by a refusal.' Every refusal reduced and stunted you. She soon discovered that to preserve your dignity in life, you learned not to want. The first lesson of survival in the family: just adjust and everything would be fine. If you learned to adjust to pain, hunger, suffering and loneliness without a single murmur of protest, you would be praised as the perfect woman, the worthy wife. But all said and done, her family was fond of her and praised her. What more could a woman want?

As her mind wandered to the matter of lust, she was distressed, wondering why men were so greedy. Why didn't they value what they held in their hands? Why did they yearn and seek ghee when they had a lovely chunk of golden butter in their palms? And they so easily forgot that all that was left at the end of their greed was charred ghee and butter which had soured, yellowed and dripped away. Fit to be thrown into the drain. The smell of rancid butter assaulted her nostrils. She sighed wearily and drifted into an uneasy sleep again.

7

After Pankaja left Pondavakkam for her in-laws' house it was as if there was a dark cloud hanging over Rajamma's home. The only *kuthu vilakku* that had brightened the house with her smiles and her chatter had been snatched away.

Pattamma, always the practical one, said to her mother, 'Why don't we also go back to Madras, Amma? That would be better for the child. There is a large house, and we have tenants. We can manage with the rent. You can lease out your acre and come once in a while to collect the yield. Leave Chinnamma here to mind the house. That way, the house will be open whenever you return and she will have a roof over her head as well.'

Rajamma agreed. Apart from the emptiness that Pankaja's departure had caused, there was the Madras property, which could not be left too long in the hands of others to be managed. And the village was becoming too claustrophobic. Madras, being a city, would be an easier place to breathe in peace.

Soon, they boarded a train for Madras with the child and a few modest belongings. Entrusting their aunt's welfare to well-meaning neighbours, they set forth to a new and uncertain future. In Pattamma's house, life soon seemed to return to normal. After a few days of sullen silence and hostile looks, the tenants began to behave courteously. Pattamma's intelligence, her practical approach, her knowledge of public affairs and her imperious bearing put the tenants in their place. They realised that they could not ignore this young woman, who was far too confident and well-read to be pushed around or dismissed as a mere helpless young widow.

Pattamma promptly got things fixed in the house, drew clear boundaries for the tenants and set in place rules that made it easier for the families to live comfortably without getting in each other's way, making the best use of the limited facilities available. There was a well in the middle of the courtyard and a hand pump for municipal water. While each family had its own bathroom, the courtyard for washing pots, pans and clothes was common. The toilets too were shared.

Pattamma's planning made it possible for tenants

to use the facilities without clashing. She occupied the first floor which had two rooms, a hall and a covered passage, which opened to the back stairs that led to the kitchen and bath on the ground floor. The space was ample and the modest rents from the other two tenants, who had a couple of rooms and a courtyard on the ground floor, made life comfortable.

Within a month, Pattama's guests resumed their visits and the heated discussions and political comments began again—leaving the tenants agape. She was fond of reading and listening to the news and her general knowledge was considerable. Besides, her visitors were not ordinary men or mere merchants or priests. They were lawyers, teachers, students and political leaders. And her neighbours were in awe of this determined and unusual young woman. Her only concession to widowhood was that she wore no flowers or jewels or *kumkum*. She marched around the house, her trailing *pallu* flung over her right shoulder, or untucked, free flowing. Her gleaming high forehead was bare of *kumkum*.

Not all the jewels in the world could have added a whit to her grace. Pattamma could keep her visitors entertained with her discussion of politics and literature. Her haughty and ironic demeanour was an armour to deal with any busybody, who might try and advise or discipline her. Strangely enough, her house was not labelled or perceived as a house of ill repute. Just one that bewildered the ordinary householder, filling him with awe. This was perhaps due to her political awareness and her outspoken behaviour. She did not conduct herself as a helpless young widow should but was authoritative and firm in all her dealings with people.

It was a period of upheaval with talk of the country's independence filling the air. Satyagraha was in the making and Gandhiji was calling on women to come forth and free their motherland. Narrow domestic walls had begun to crumble and women, charged with the excitement of fighting to set their motherland free, began to flood meetings and protests. What could be nobler than fighting to free Mother India? Gandhiji had called them and inspired them to take action. So, Pattamma also began to go out for a few meetings.

One constant visitor to her house was a communist leader called Comrade Iyengar. He had spent some months underground to avoid the authorities. He was related to her niece Chudi, and so, he had taken refuge in Pattamma's house. His presence was very important to her growth. She spent all her free time with him, listening to him expound communist philosophy and the importance of revolution. He spoke of the dictatorship, of the proletariat, and the ideas he shared shaped Pattamma's tender mind, enlarging her understanding of society and the world.

Suddenly, her widowhood and traditional beliefs became unimportant and faded into the background. Her intellectual growth during this time was enormous. The political issues of Satyagraha, freedom and self-respect seized her mind, freeing it from the fetters of fate and orthodoxy. The shell of the child widow and her miserable fate cracked, and a new, free woman was hatched.

Comrade Iyengar continued to visit her and spend plenty of time arguing with her about politics. There was a strong bond between them. He continued to be a liberating factor for Pattamma. He told her about how the peasant women in Telangana had made history by taking up arms against the Razakars and the Nizam who were exploiting them. Listening to stories of women carrying guns, entering forests, leaving their children behind and fighting for their survival stirred her deeply. While she could not leave behind the narrow domestic walls which confined her, her keen mind, set free, soared across the sky, searching for the meaning of freedom.

Comrade Iyengar also introduced her to Periyar's ideas. Reading and listening to these concepts liberated her from the stranglehold of orthodoxy. It restored her self-respect and her dignity. Periyar seemed to speak directly to her heart. Comrade Iyengar was busy organising the harbour workers in Madras and he also talked to her constantly of their exploitation. She suggested that he should set up a store for the harbour workers, which would provide them with all their needs at cost price and also offer credit. He took her advice and set up the Harbour Workers' Union Office and store in Bhagat House. They were well-matched emotionally and intellectually, and provided each other a mutually supportive companionship.

Periyar's words about women's equality and the oppression of caste traditions were causing much turbulence among the orthodox. She read about and listened to his ideas with interest. He helped her to make sense of her situation and gave her the courage to be herself. Although given her background she could not put into practice his opinions about caste, everything he said about women and marriage struck a chord in her. It made her feel different, special, and brave enough to live a life free of guilt and shame.

Her intelligence and wit drew together a group of talented professionals including lawyers, doctors and journalists who were at her beck and call. These gatherings at her house, where coffee and space were liberally available, went on to become a regular affair.

She ran a kind of salon regally, though she had neither wealth nor position. She listened to the radio, read the newspapers and discussed the merits and demerits of the salt Satyagraha or non-cooperation heatedly with her visitors. And her intelligence, courage and conviction carried the day.

The freedom struggle altered many set ways. The country was in the throes of change. It was a new day. A new dawn. The news of protests, thrashings and arrests poured in. Gandhi announced Satyagraha. Women and students devoted themselves to the struggle. The radio was the centrepiece of most homes. Pattamma longed to go and join the protests with the students. But she had no companion to go with and she was already being watched hawk-like by her orthodox neighbours. Besides, there was young Rajappa. She could not risk his safety or his future.

Rajappa, as he was affectionately called, was thoroughly spoilt by all his mother's friends. They competed with each other to heap gifts and praise on him. Pattamma's beauty, intelligence and demeanour ensured that mother and son were not objects of pity or exploitation. She looked positively regal as she sat on the large wooden swing in the middle of the hall, fanning herself with a palm leaf fan.

Sometimes, the smile flitting on her lips would

be replaced by a slight frown of concentration as she listened to their accounts of the world outside. Though she rarely stepped out of the confines of her home, her mind was occupied with all the struggles and meetings taking place across the city. She was a new woman in her thinking, though she never once crossed the threshold of her house.

8

Rajappa shot up quickly. Gentle and soft-spoken, his sensitive face always drew the attention of the older boys in school. They called out to him roughly, but stroked his cheek or ruffled his hair gently. Rajappa felt a prick of pleasure when they did that.

He loved his aunt Pankaja, who visited them every year during the summer holidays. It was a pleasure to see his cousins Chellappa, Ramji and bright-eyed Chudi. But his aunt Pankaja was the most precious of all. She loved him dearly, laid no conditions on him unlike his mother, and cherished him. One day, he came home early and overheard her arguing with his mother.

She said, 'I think it's wrong. You should think about the child. He is at a vulnerable age. He mustn't get hurt.'

His mother dismissed this remark right away. The two of them promptly changed the subject when they saw him. He vaguely guessed what it was about. He had often seen his mother vanish into the room above the cellar when Varadan appeared in the afternoon. After half an hour, she would emerge, slightly breathless, wiping her face with her *pallu*. Then Varadan would slip out quietly without stepping into the house. Some days, it would be Krishnan. A couple of times, it was Mohan. He hadn't quite understood what it was all about except that it was a topic best avoided. A few tenants in the house looked curious, but they dared not raise the subject with Pattamma, who was as imperious as a queen.

Although she wore her sari traditionally with the pleats drawn between her legs and tucked behind, she left her *pallu* trailing or flung over her shoulder, never making an attempt to cover her bare right shoulder and bare back. Poised and slender, she was a picture of grace. Not self-conscious at all, she was aware of the figure she struck, and seldom glanced at a mirror except to comb her hair in the morning. The loose knot fell open by mid-morning and her hair lay in waves across her back. She was careless about her looks as only a real beauty who is also intelligent could afford to be. She liked to read. She did not seek approval in the eyes of those who were watching her nor did she heed their sullen resentment. They did not approve of her non-conformity but lacked the courage to confront her.

Rajappa stood by her and went about his work. He did well in his studies and he also loved to play cricket. After completing his graduation, he decided to study law. Pattamma's health had begun to decline. She developed diabetes and huge dark patches appeared on her flawless skin. She felt hot and breathless and began to have palpitations. She constantly twirled her palm leaf fan to soothe the itching and burning patches that marred her once golden skin.

She soon realised that she could not manage the house without help. So, when Rajappa was still in law college, a desperate Pattamma decided they needed family support and fixed his marriage with the daughter of a distant cousin of hers. Pankaja had moved to Secunderabad and had her hands full.

Pattamma felt vulnerable. She was anxious to ensure Rajappa's future and she felt that her son needed companionship as well as the support of his in-laws. They had no extended family to turn to after all. Rajappa tried to protest saying he wanted to finish his studies but Pattamma imperiously dismissed his objections and fixed the marriage.

There were about thirty people, including family members, a few neighbours and tenants at the bride's house for the ill-fated marriage ceremony. The tuneless trumpets and the cacophony of the drums added little glamour to the miserable event. Rajappa, tall, fair and good-looking, towered over the bride who was short, plump and plain. The marriage ceremony got over, the guests ate their fill and left. Pattamma sat for a while with Pankaja, who had come for the wedding, trying to discuss future plans with the bride's father.

Sundaram was a petty man, bustling with self-importance and completely unaware of Pattamma's capability. Proud of having clinched a propertied and good-looking son-in-law without any inkling of what the future held, he boasted about his good fortune and was dismissive of Pattamma. Rajappa watched quietly.

The bride, Lakshmi, had studied up to her F.A; a great achievement in those days. She also played the violin reasonably well. She was short, stocky and rather plain-looking, but Pattamma who was looking for an alliance that would support her, a single widow without extended family, was satisfied. She had to complete one more examination and it was agreed that she would remain in her mother's house until she finished it. Pattamma valued education and music and was very happy to have an educated daughter-in-law.

Meanwhile, predictably, fate played its part. An epidemic of small pox broke out and Lakshmi suffered a virulent attack, which left her scarred and badly disfigured. Rajappa used to visit his wife's house regularly on his mother's command. Unfortunately, his father-in-law and brother-in-law were vicious and grasping men. They suffered from the arrogance and the meanness that gilded the sense of superiority, which marked most average middle-class Brahmins who had no other distinction to boast of but caste. When he said in a subdued tone that his mother had suggested that they send her daughter-in-law home, they mocked him crudely.

'Home? You call that a home? And you call yourself a man? You? A widow's son! Brought up by three widows! What will you do there? Pack your bags and move into this house and we will make a man of you.'

Rajappa, young and sensitive, suffered their insults in silence. Gradually, he simply stopped visiting them and after a year, his father-in-law was forced to swallow his pride and send his daughter to her husband's house. Rajappa was scrupulously polite but distant with her. He never had any physical contact with her. His mother raged about this and kept sending the girl to his room, inventing excuses. He was patient and courteous but he did not touch his wife despite his mother's efforts. His mother felt that all the humiliation heaped on him by his father-in-law and brother-in-law had affected him.

Though she was furious at him, she knew that this abstinence was the result of the insults he had been forced to suffer. If only he would stop being so stubborn and give her a grandchild! She fumed but could do nothing to change his stance. He smiled patiently, listening to her with his head bent, and then went about his work as usual. Old mother Rajamma died peacefully in her sleep a year later. Her troubles had ended. But Pattamma felt her mother's loss keenly.

9

Lakshmi was her mild and quiet self. She carried out the household work dutifully, lighting the fire under the huge copper cauldron in the bathroom and pumping the tap water in the courtyard for cooking. She served the mother and son their meals and also cleaned the house meticulously. She worked hard every day without complaining. In the afternoon, Pattamma would ask Lakshmi to play the violin for a while. Then, she would read a novel or magazine for some time. At four, Lakshmi would go down to make a tumbler of coffee for her mother-in-law and herself and some tiffin, either idlis or upma. Lakshmi and Pattamma would eat together. She was not a great cook but Pattamma, who was normally demanding, would eat quietly. Rajappa would arrive later, only eating at home sometimes. Most days, he would have eaten out with his friends. Lakshmi would sigh and put away his share for the maid's breakfast.

The maid was an old woman called Kuppu, who came in the morning to sweep the front yard. She would sprinkle water on it before drawing a few sad lines on the ground with rice flour. Kuppu was a thin, dark woman who wore earrings that dangled from her elongated lobes. She was devoted to Pattamma. Sometimes, Lakshmi too would take the rice flour and draw an elaborate design in the courtyard. Her mother-in-law always took pains to praise her drawing and her music. But her praise just bounced off Lakshmi. What use was her mother-in-law's praise when her husband never came anywhere near her?

Lakshmi kept silent about it, but she was deeply conscious of the cruel fact that she cut a pitiful figure beside her tall, handsome husband. The rare ritual which involved them standing side by side as a couple humiliated and wounded her. Rajappa was blissfully unconscious of how bad things were. He was always matter of fact with her. When she snapped back at some routine question he raised, a faint frown would appear on his forehead. It would vanish in a second.

He was aware that the sexual distance between them troubled her but there was nothing he could do about it. Nothing was going to make him behave differently towards his wife.

Rajappa was busy with his practice and his cricket

association. It was there that he found satisfaction. He was mild and soft-spoken but incredibly stubborn. He had built a good practice with the clients that his mother's friends and admirers sent his way and he devoted his time and energy to growing it.

The minute Rajappa returned from court at four, Seenu, a youth who lived down the street, would arrive and whistle a tune. Rajappa's face would glow when he saw Seenu. He would gift Seenu a warm smile and invite him in. Rajappa's expression would soften the minute Seenu appeared, and throwing an arm across his shoulder he would draw Seenu close. Seenu would saunter around the house while Rajappa finished his work and then the two would wander off for a few hours to the terrace or the thatched hut on the terrace, cooled by the sea breeze.

Pattamma saw Seenu as a distraction but did not grasp the depth of the bond her son shared with him. She inwardly fumed at her son for not consummating his marriage. One grandchild was all she wanted. Just one to carry on the family name! But Rajappa, so dutiful and caring otherwise, simply would not oblige her. He preferred Seenu's company over his wife's proximity.

10

The Kandala family into which Pankaja had married had three daughters and two sons. The younger son, Sampath, Gopalan's brother, had been given away in adoption to a propertied cousin. All three daughters had been married off well. The parents had done their duty but there is such a thing as fate. Unfortunately, two of the daughters had been widowed, one, after bearing a daughter, and the other before she reached puberty. The older daughter, Kuppamma, was very frail when she was an infant. So, her mother had placed her on a heap of rubbish and her grandmother picked her up. From then on, she was called 'Kuppa' (rubbish). Thus, they believed she would escape the evil eye and survive.

When she was eleven, she was married off to a Brahmin priest. She bore him a daughter named Kannamma (dear one). Kuppamma doted on her daughter and had many dreams for her future. But her husband died of typhoid when the child was four. Kuppamma was reduced to the status of a shaven widow. The machinations of fate! Who can change the writing on a mortal's forehead? Kuppa was intelligent, a deft manager, a good cook and she could fix almost anything. She was also incredibly light fingered and untroubled by any scruples whatsoever. As a result, the rest of the family kept a careful watch on the jewellery and silverware at home.

Once, she simply removed and disposed of a dozen large silver plates in which the men and children used to eat. The family went into shock. 'Maybe the monkeys took them,' she said airily. While monkeys no doubt roamed freely and stole food and other articles from the outer rooms, the courtyard and the spot near the well, it was impossible for them to enter the store room where the heavy plates were stacked. But Kuppa was a daughter of the family. And there was nothing to be done. There were a few murmurs and the matter was forgotten.

The younger daughter was good-looking and so she was named Singaramma (the beautiful one). A child widow, she lost her husband before she had even looked at his face. Singaramma was just nine years old when she was married off to Varahan who was fourteen at the time. The marriage seemed to be cursed from the very beginning. Uncle Chamappa who had gone mad and had spent the previous at burning ghats and burial grounds learning black magic turned up at the marriage ceremony. He was a hoary and frightful sight. He was furious that he had not been informed or been invited to his niece's marriage. He waved his bag around, shouting, 'Why wasn't I told? Am I not an uncle?'

The men of the family tried their best to pacify him and prevent a scene.

'No, Chamappa, we sent Raman for you. But you were not to be found anywhere!' they said.

Chamappa was enraged and swung his bag wildly. Out of it tumbled a frightening assortment of knives and sickles. Somehow, the men managed to calm him down and drag him away to the dining space. All the relatives were shocked by the uncle's outburst. The weapons and the threat of violence were sickening. What kind of omen was this for a young couple's wedding? Anyway, slowly peace was restored and innocent Singaramma was taken to her parents' home. She played and sang without a care in the world. The ugly incident involving her uncle was soon forgotten. Within two years of the wedding, before she had even come of age, her young groom, Varahan, died of typhoid.

Singaramma kept playing. The parents did not put pressure on her and make a fuss. Thus, blissfully unaware of her newly widowed status, Singaramma set off one Dussehra to visit the neighbours and collect the *paan* and fruit that guests were offered. She came back with her bag full and her mother and aunts were shocked at this calamity. They started to shout at her saying that she was a widow and had no right to visit on festive occasions. She looked puzzled at first. Then she screamed at them and insisted that she would keep visiting. The agitated women grabbed her, gave her a thrashing, stripped off her blouse and removed her nose ring. She grew quiet and began to register the fact that she was now a widow. She would not be allowed to live like other girls.

One day, her mother sent her to buy some oil from the shop down the street. When she got there, she suddenly found that she could not speak. She kept grimacing and gasping, unable to say a single word. They took her to a doctor who confirmed that she had suffered an attack of facial paralysis. The pretty, chirpy Singaramma was transformed into a disfigured widow. Fate is cruelly ironic. It works in its own harsh ways. Singaramma's stroke caused one eyelid to droop, and her mouth to twist slightly. Her face, mouth and drooping eye seemed to mock the name her mother had so lovingly given her. Ill-tempered and moody, she grumbled constantly, refusing to accept her widowhood or her paralysis in a proper spirit of resignation. She raged against her fate.

Soon, Singaramma came of age and the family told her that now she would have to get her head shaved and wear widow's whites. To their utter horror, she refused to do so flatly. 'If you want me to shave my head, write an acre of land in my name so that I don't have to come every month to you begging for two rupees to pay the barber,' she demanded. Shocked at her temerity and the audacity of her claim, the family backed off and Singaramma kept her hair the way it was and continued to wear coloured saris and earrings. She gave up her nose ring and her blouse as a concession to a dead husband she had never set eyes on since the marriage ceremony.

She was incorrigible, fussy and ill-tempered and the rest of the family steered clear of her. At times, she was humorous, making vulgar jokes about the men in the family and their weaknesses, which tickled the other women who dared not laugh out aloud. Her hair was always dishevelled, a couple of locks framing her face, adding to her slightly crazy look. Having been cheated by fate, she was inconsiderate and fussy, much to the dismay of her mother and sisters.

To add to her sorrows, Singaramma suffered from chronic constipation and spent most of her day walking to and from the lavatory at the far end of the yard. She had to carry a bucket of water with her. The lavatory was just four walls with an opening for the door. No roof. No water. The women usually left the bucket at the entrance to indicate it was occupied. Sometimes, two women would enter together, sitting opposite each other on the raised platform that ran around the latrine, chatting away. The open walls were generally occupied by monkeys that gibbered and stared at the squatting women. Meanwhile, pigs wandered in and lapped away at the fresh shit. The women had learned to ignore them. Trying to shoo away the monkeys or pigs meant they would be taking on the risk of being bitten.

The men, chewing neem sticks, wandered off to the canal bank farther down and washed themselves there. They joked around, discussed business matters and the communal shit was an enjoyable social activity for them. The monkeys perched on the trees watched curiously and jabbered away. Sometimes, if one of the men tried to shoo off a monkey it would growl ferociously. A monkey bite could be fatal and so the men learnt to tolerate their chatter.

There were some nights when one heard a rustle and a grunt in the hall where they all slept. Rajamannar, the father who was in his 50s, still needed sex but his wife was far too ashamed to submit to his demands with two widowed daughters in the house. She had stopped wearing flowers and bright silks after they came home. So, Rajamannar sulked and slunk off in the afternoon to a widowed sister-in-law who was only too willing to spread her legs at siesta time. And so, life went on and everyone made their peace with it.

Sampath, the younger son, had been given away to a childless cousin who needed a son to perform his last rites. He always resented the fact that he had been put up for adoption so easily. He lived in a separate, small portion of the house. He was a Licensed Medical Practitioner and had a modest practice. His wife, Kamala, was a beauty with jet black hair, big black eyes and clear, fair skin. She bore a child every year and had no help to speak of. Surrounded by a dozen children with a million different demands, she was exhausted, ill-tempered and unkempt. She looked beautiful though dishevelled. And her children grew and flourished in spite of her fatigue.

Since her husband had been adopted and he had also disputed the family property claims, she was not entitled to any help from the widowed aunts or women in his original family. And no support was forthcoming. Unfailingly, when she felt her labour pains coming on, she would fill a thermos with black coffee to sip between her contractions, and cook a large meal of rice, vegetable curry and rasam for the children. Calling for Raju's bullock cart, which was always tied up across the street, she would set off alone, carrying her bundle of clothes and her flask to the Mission Hospital in town. Kamala would deliver the baby easily and painlessly and be back home on the third day. Her husband would manage the cooking and the children for a couple of weeks and she would resume her duties after. Beset by scampering children and unending housework, Kamala was always exhausted and despairing.

One afternoon, she sat wearily beside the well and moaned, 'All the time I hear people saying, "Poor thing, her child died! Poor thing, what sorrow!" about so many other women in this town. Won't my ears ever be soothed by the sound of someone saying, "Poor Kamala! She lost a child!" It is my endless misfortune that none of these devils will ever die.'

Her mother-in-law, hearing her, clicked her tongue and shooed her into the house, 'Stupid girl! Don't talk like that. These are not things to say loudly even when you are troubled.'

Kamala's sisters-in-law chuckled at her desperation. Each had her measure of troubles and no sympathy to waste on poor Kamala, who delivered a child every year. Her eldest was a girl called Mohana. A pretty, dark beauty. Then came Krishnan who was bright and smart, followed by Vaidehi, skinny and gawky. After that, even Kamala seemed to lose count of the endless succession of flasks of black coffee she had carried to sip during labour. She had seven children in all. They ran around half-naked, playing happily, seldom cleanly bathed and fresh. They were healthy though and enjoyed chasing the monkeys and pigs that were found in large numbers in the backyard. They just proved the saying that all you really need to rear a child is a handful of rice and a large heart.

11

Pankaja smiled sadly in her sleep as she dreamt of Kamala's children and her plight. They could have been friends but Sampath, who coveted a share of the main property, had cut off all cordial relations with the rest of his family. Strange family indeed, where the son was an enemy and the pretty grandchildren were denied the comfort of loving aunts and grandparents all because of a piece of property! She had tried to speak to Kamala when they were both washing clothes at the well, but there was a stern call from either Sampath or her mother-in-law to stop gossiping. You had to lie on the bed that was made by others in your life! There was no escape. You could never make your own bed. If you could do that, you could always adjust it to suit your needs. If you had that freedom where was the need for sorrow? Or regret?

12

It was a warm, cloudy day in August. Singaramma was feeling dull and her stomach was heavy and bloated. Unable to bear her distress, she picked up a jute bag and set off to buy some herbs and medicines. Her constipation was really troubling, but no one at home had any sympathy for her. They just joked when she complained about her distress or tried to seek help. They did not understand the torture of having a gut that she could not empty no matter how hard she grunted. It was impractical for her to take a purgative daily and so she suffered. What wouldn't she give to be able to clean out her bowels completely! What a blessed relief that would be! What unbearable lightness of being!

As she was walking along the street, musing, a bullock cart rattled by. She peered into it and saw a familiar face. It was a Muslim woman with her earlobes pierced all over, wearing black kajal, and her lips red with the *paan* she was chewing. Her sari was drawn over her head but her face was visible. The woman saw her and turned away quickly. There was something oddly familiar about that face and Singaramma racked her brains to place her. Suddenly, she realised that it was Mangai from the house on the back street. Mangai's husband, who was old and sick, had died six months ago. Her head was shaved and she was stripped of her jewels and her clothes, and given an unbleached white sari to wear. She had gone through the grim rites quietly.

One night, she had disappeared with her clothes and jewels. Gone without a trace. First, the family thought she must have gone down to the river. It was only hours later that they realised her things were missing. They searched for her in a few nearby houses but could not track her. By then, it was too late to do anything because she had been gone for long and they dared not go to the police because of the scandal it would cause.

So, this was the secret! Mangai had run away with a Muslim. Muslims oddly did not mind if a woman was a widow. They were not keen on finding virgin brides. And so, they were seen as a menace by upper-caste Hindus. Singaramma felt a twinge of pain in her heart. If only her face had not been disfigured, she too might have had a chance of starting a new life. What in this world could be worse than being a child widow in a Brahmin house? And in the name of some rebirth in a distant future, she would continue to suffer the anger and contempt of this unsympathetic family, who believed she was paying the price for her sins in her last life.

Her face twitched sharply and it was clouded with anger.

It was not as if young widows were safe and protected in their families. Wasn't it only last month that Kanakamma from the third house on the back street had set off to Benares on a pilgrimage with young Tilakam, her nephew's widow? Tilakam was only sixteen and shapely. Even her unbleached sari could not hide her full breasts and hips. Singaramma too longed to go along and see Benares and bathe in the Ganga. She was shot down quickly.

She had overheard the older women talking. There was a Mission Hospital in Benares. After a few dips in the river and visits to the temple the young woman would be taken there. She would deliver safely. The missionaries would be glad to keep the child and save one more soul for Christ.

The mother would bathe in the Ganges after giving birth, go around the temple, and cleansed of her sins, she would return home to resume her household chores. The young widow's work was indispensable to a large household especially when the other daughters-in-law visited their mother's homes or were caught up in childbirth or were busy nursing their sick husbands.

Singaramma, being obstinate and disfigured, suffered neither from overwork nor assault. She was a law unto herself. The men and the women in the family gave her a wide berth to escape her tirades.

13

It was the month of Purattassi. The Kanadala house had been washed and cleaned. The annual ceremony of Varadaraja Iyengar, the father of Rajamannar, was to take place the next day. The women had cleaned the kitchen and removed all traces of cooked food or liquids which would pollute it. In the morning, the male cooks would arrive, strip off their shirts, and after a quick bath near the well, enter the kitchen wearing wet towels around their waists, which had turned grey with use. With their sacred threads, soiled and dangling, they would take over the place, swiftly peeling and chopping yams, slicing *vendakkai* (ladies' finger), soaking dal for the crisp vadas, and breaking up the jaggery for the *payasam* (dessert).

The ceremonial meal for death-related rites could not include anything but traditional foods. So, green chillies, tomatoes, potatoes, lemons and fresh coriander were excluded. So was turmeric and tuvar dal. Instead, the meal included yams, *vendakkai*, bittergourd, snakegourd, black pepper, asafoetida and jaggery. The meal was rich grey in colour and different. The ceremonial offering to the dead man was then put out on a banana leaf for the cow. The ceremony took about an hour and the priests were given their *dakshinas* (fees) of brass pots, towels, dhotis and cash.

After the Brahmins had eaten their fill and burped to their content, the men in the family were served. Then the cooks sat in the kitchen and hastily finished their meal. The women ate in the end, laughing and joking as they enjoyed the special peppery dishes. For once, they had no work except to clear up after the cooks left. Any leftovers had to be fed to a cow or mixed with ash to render them uneatable by unclean animals or human beings, and thrown away.

Amrutha was an old aunt who was half blind and deaf. She generally moved around through the year from temple to temple, watching the rituals and living on the *prasadam* that was offered to the gods at these holy places. That year, she came home in time for her father's ceremony. In the evening, she ate some of the food that was given to her and rested against the wooden pillar in front of the house. After it grew dark and the family members began to go to bed, she picked up her mat and wandered into the backyard, searching for the stone bench on which washed clothes and pots were usually kept.

Her bones ached at the thought of lying on the ground and heaving herself up again. She could hardly see in the dark and she felt her way to the bench. Then, she spread out her mat and stretched out. She wondered vaguely why there was a curve to the bench as she lay down. But it did not bother her. She fell asleep at once and rolled over.

The house was buzzing with activity and no one missed Aunt Amrutha. The cooks drew water from the well and all the ceremonies went off smoothly. At night, the women noticed that she was missing. Assuming that she was lost on the street, they sent a couple of boys to look for her. The boys looked for her in a few houses and came back empty-handed. The household went on with its daily activities as usual. Three days later, when Sampath was drawing water from the well, his bucket got entangled in something. Thinking it was a sari that had fallen into the well, he cursed and peeped in. Startled at what he saw down there, he called out and all the men and women came rushing out. They asked a Yenadhi lad to climb down into the well. He found her body curled up and caught in a wedge of a rock inside the well.

The funeral was swift. Aunt Amrutha had no children of her own to grieve. For a week, they drew their water from the neighbour's well and had their well dredged and cleaned. The thought that for two days they had been drinking the water in which a dead woman lay sent waves of nausea through the family. But there was no grief or shock for the woman who lay trapped in the water for two days. She was an old, barren widow after all.

14

Pankaja had delivered her first two children, a son and a daughter, at the Kandala home in Nellore. Her mother being alone and poor, her husband decided that her deliveries should take place in Nellore. He travelled but there were enough widowed aunts to help his mother. Rajamma came for the deliveries, but being orthodox she could only cook for her daughter and eat the leftovers. Custom and orthodoxy did not permit her to eat the food cooked by women of another *gotra* (clan). She was given a separate fire.

She cooked soft rice and greens and peppered vegetables for Pankaja. She was given a glass of buttermilk, which she served her daughter and diluted and drank herself. She ate the leftover food she had cooked and washed up the pots near the well. The large backyard was like a forest and she could always find fresh vegetables and greens for her daughter. After twenty-one days, Pankaja could eat the family meal with a few restrictions and Rajamma made do with some rice and thin buttermilk and a chutney of coarsely ground fresh *karepak* (curry) leaves, dry red chillies, and some tamarind and salt.

She craved a tumbler of hot coffee in the afternoon but this family did not drink coffee. She was far too ashamed to mention her need for coffee. Imagine a widow having needs! That too after, even her eldest daughter, had been widowed so young. Besides, coffee was considered impure by the orthodox. Some families however, roasted and ground their own coffee. Like Rajamma's. But this was also considered unorthodox and alien.

15

The years passed quickly and it was time for Gopalan to leave Nellore. He was posted as the jail doctor in Madurai. They had a pleasant quarter with a pretty garden full of jasmine and roses. In the backyard, there was a vegetable patch where Pankaja grew some greens, *vendakkai* and *avarai* (green beans). She always had fresh vegetables from her backyard though the warden sent them a good supply from the jail purchases. It was September, the season of rain, and Pankaja was already expecting her third child. Gopalan decided that she could deliver at the Madurai Hospital and asked his mother and mother-in-law to come over and manage things. Rajamma used to make the dishes her daughter's diet specified and eat the leftovers. Lakshmiamma used to cook for herself and her son.

Till the day of her delivery, Pankaja had cooked and served both her mother-in-law and her mother. The two women could eat Pankaja's cooking since she was both daughter and daughter-in-law. After she gave birth to a baby boy, the older women cooked for themselves and their respective children. At the end of forty days and the ritual purification after child birth, Pankaja resumed her duties in the kitchen with the grandmothers taking turns minding the children.

Another month passed and both mother and mother-in-law left by train with an escort. Pankaja managed her household and three children well. As the baby grew, the prisoners who worked in the doctor's garden adored him and played with him. His sweetness and mischief lightened their dreary days.

16

In the Kandala home, unlike Singaramma, Kuppamma was an intelligent person and a useful presence. She had high hopes for her only daughter, Kannamma, who was a petite, dark child. She went to school and had a clear melodious voice so her mother arranged music lessons for her. In order to fulfil her own unfulfilled desires, she would light some incense, place flowers in the music room, and keep a warm glass of milk for the tutor. This brought on snorts of contempt from her sisters. Was this a Dasi house? What was wrong with Kuppa? But Kuppamma had a vicious tongue and not even her mother dared to oppose her. They would gossip that at this rate, the girl would elope with the music tutor. But perhaps, because she was small-built and mousy, that did not happen.

In good time, Kuppamma fixed Kannamma's marriage to a cousin called Sundaram, who was a lawyer. After the marriage, the couple moved to Madras so Sundaram could practice. Kannamma continued practising her music. She bore him five children, two girls and three boys. Sundaram, who had a wild sense of humour, was notoriously tight-fisted. His dream was to be a *koteeshwaran* (millionaire) He would add up all his assets to calculate whether he was worth a crore. His miserliness was a joke in the whole family. When they teased him about his stinginess, he would grow furious and ask how many *choultries* Anna Sampath had built where Thambi Sundaram had not dug wells? Count!

Kannamma earned small sums of money by singing at temple concerts and festivals. She was a good singer though not greatly gifted. But there was a steady demand for her performances at regular events. She had a mridangam player, who accompanied her in all her performances, shaking his head while she trilled. She was able to make a modest sum of money from her concerts. After some years, Kannamma had had enough of a respectable life. Family, five children and a stingy husband did not fulfil her needs. One day, she packed a bag and left to live with the mridangam player, the *maddaliga* (drummer) as the family contemptuously referred to him. He was a pariah and the whole community reeled in horror. To add insult to injury, she lived openly with him in a hut in the *cheri* (slum), sending waves of horror through the Brahmins, aunts, cousins and extended family living in Madras.

This was a *cheri* on the banks of the Buckingham Canal, between Narasimhapuram and Luz Corner. All the shops, hotels, banks and bus stops were in Luz. Soon, her relatives stopped taking the shortcut through the *cheri* and began crossing the bridge and walking along the Kapalishwaran Temple Tank Road. Or, they took the longer path across Abhiramapuram, the colony behind the *cheri*. The shame of seeing her sitting cheerfully on the doorstep of her hut, her hair loose, sipping the tea she had bought from a tea vendor, was humiliating. She was utterly shameless, looking straight at them and not even making an attempt to hide her face or look away. '*Aiyyo! Karmame! Jyeshte! Jyeshte!*' (What a terrible fate! Disgusting! Disgusting!) They muttered, shuddering in revulsion and horror.

She simply sat sunning herself, gazing at them idly. They were terrified that she might actually greet them in front of the whole *cheri*. To tell the truth, she had no interest in them, though she might have enjoyed embarrassing them for a lark. Sometimes, when they took the Kapalishwar Tank Road, they would see her sitting at a roadside cafe near the temple sharing a glass of tea with her *maddaliga*.

'Filthy wretch! Why doesn't she drop dead? Can't

she even buy herself a cup of tea? How obscene!' They exclaimed, shocked by her brazenness.

What was most disgusting about this woman was that she had flung so much dirty linen into the public. Everyone knew that life must go on. Countless housewives, after sending their husbands off to work, would quickly wash, change into a bright-coloured sari, comb their hair, braid jasmine flowers—carefully wrapped in a damp cloth at night—into their hair, smear some sandalwood on their throats, darken their eyes and slip out for a morning show. In the middle of the show, they would disappear for an hour with a companion into a nearby lodge.

Returning home, they would quickly tuck a wad of notes into their trunks and change back into the plain sari of the morning. As they washed their hands and feet, they would carefully wash out traces of sandalwood and retie their hair into sober knots. Sometimes, a nosy neighbour would shout, 'Mami! How was the cinema?' The woman would smile, and placing a finger on her lips, shush her. But that was life and a question of survival. Money was hard to earn and life was difficult. But these women did not defy custom and tradition. They did not spit in the face of caste norms. As long as one was discreet and careful, people were tolerant. This brazen defiance of caste and tradition was intolerable.

But alas, this was not a community known for physical violence. They had manipulated the violence of other communities to their advantage through their learning, but they lacked the muscle to directly squash Kannamma like a cockroach. They could not grind her into the dust.

Kannamma, however, was content for the first time in her life. She had borne five children to the husband who clasped her clumsily and finished before she even knew what was happening. Her *maddaliga* played his expert rhythms on her thin body, striking chords and conjuring up a delight she had never tasted in her twenty years of marriage. Never having known the pleasures of the flesh, she adored him. He expected nothing much from her. Though she was small and thin, the fact that she was educated, could sing and earn some money and accept his life as it was, was enough. They ate together. However, since she could not eat the dry fish or the beef he enjoyed, he always brought her a small packet of idli-sambar and buttermilk, or a plate of vadas. She was content.

They talked about their concerts, the sabhas and how much they would pay, and the songs that were most popular. To the sabhas, she wore the Brahmin *madisar* sari and they arrived separately at different times, never as a couple. They were polite and formal to each other in public, knowing the sabhas were dominated by

Brahmins who would cut off their livelihood if they came to know. Since the extended family was too ashamed and disgusted to gossip except among themselves, they were fairly secure. Kannamma was happy for the first time in her life, finding companionship and the kind of sex that she had never experienced in her conventional marriage. She would have liked her children to keep in touch, but she was not willing to give up the deep contentment she had finally found, for the sake of her children.

One day, Kannamma was sitting on the doorstep, enjoying the faint sea breeze, oblivious of the stench rising from the Buckingham canal and the faint odour of dry fish and offal cooking that pervaded the *cheri*. She rarely missed the scent of the incense or the sandalwood that had been such a constant presence at home, thanks to her mother's meticulousness. Suddenly, she began to hum to herself:

> *Lakshmi kalyanam vaibhogame! Sita kalyanam vaibhogame!*
> (Oh, the grandeur of Lakshmi's wedding! Oh, the grandeur of Sita's wedding!)

Why had that tune floated into her mind? It was the ritual song for every auspicious event—the anointing of a bride, the blessing of a girl who had just come of age, the celebration of the seventh month of a woman's first pregnancy. The whole house would echo with women's voices hitting high and low notes, quavering, melodious, creating an aura of auspiciousness. But now in her 40s, after bearing five children, living with this man in the slum, she felt the joy and satisfaction she had never dreamt of in all those years.

She drew him close as he entered the hut and stroked his muscular, swarthy hand. The hand that had uplifted her art and satisfied her flesh, as no moment in her marriage or childbirth had. He looked at her quizzically but she turned away with a smile, continuing to hum into the dusk. Soon, it was time to light the lantern. She began to trim the wick and clean the chimney, still humming the tune.

Meanwhile, her husband Sundaram, who was a lawyer, decided to shift his modest practice to the Supreme Court. He never spoke about her. Whether he left to escape the shame of living in Madras or he had actually found a decent practice in Delhi, no one knew. Sundaram, to his credit, never mentioned his wife. He neither cursed her nor complained to anyone. The dignity he maintained in this matter elevated him beyond any criticism or irony.

He was devoted to his Manni, Pankaja, and liked to regale her with tales of his practice and his adventures. One day, they were sitting together on the stone bench outside their Mylapore house. He was regaling her with stories. He told her that he had given up smoking since he had started reciting the *Vishnu Sahasranamam*.

'Manni! Why should I soil the mouth that recites to the Lord with filthy tobacco? So, I gave up.'

Pankaja nodded, amused. He drew closer and said confidentially, 'You know, Manni, I used to drink also. That drink is a wretched thing. There are different kinds. Whiskey, brandy, gin and rum. You mix it with some soda and drink it.'

His voice dropped even lower and he drew closer to her.

'Do you know, Manni, that the minute you drink, you want a woman? Any woman! Even if someone drapes a sari round a lamp post, you will fall on it. So, I gave up the habit completely.'

He paused gravely for a second and added, 'You know, even if I see a bottle of soda, now, I feel the same urge! What an evil habit!'

Pankaja nodded. She thought for a moment that with all his faults, Gopalan never touched a drop of liquor. He used to smoke in the early days in Secunderabad and she had actually liked the smell of tobacco on his lips and clothes. After a couple of years, he had given up because of the slight, persistent cough that troubled him. His cough always heralded his arrival, and whether in the hospital or at home, staff and children would quickly resume their duties. Sighing at the memory, she wiped her face with the end of her sari.

Sundaram looked at his watch and said, 'It's time to go, Manni. I have a client coming to see me.'

Pankaja thought about Sundaram's family. What needless suffering! The children and the father crushed by the disgrace of a mother and wife unburdened by any sense of duty or shame. Kannamma could have thought of the children. What did they do to deserve this burden of a mother who was held in contempt by family and community?

But life does not come to a halt even when a dear one dies. It has to go on…

Kannamma's children had grown up. The girls found jobs as clerks in a government office. The eldest son, Padmanabhan, who had suffered the most, practised as a lawyer in the Madras courts. The youngest boy developed a sudden fever and died. Through all this, Kuppamma lived with them, minding the house and cooking for the family. Whether she ever regretted her daughter's choices or considered her own role in shaping them, was anybody's guess. On the whole, her cousins and sisters-in-law tolerated her in good humour and let her live. Any criticism of her was only done behind her back.

The other sister, Rukmani, moved to her husband's home in Madurai. She lived prosperously. Her husband had a good job, owned plenty of property and her daughters were educated and married off suitably. Their only son was dark, slim and good-looking. He did not feel any need to study hard or to look for a job when he scraped through college. He could comfortably enjoy life with his charm and his father's wealth.

17

After a few years, Gopalan decided to move to Secunderabad in search of a career. Secunderabad was a cantonment town. A number of Brahmins and Mudaliars had migrated and settled down in this clean, comfortable place. The local population was mostly Anglo-Indians, Parsis and Komtis. There were a few middle-class Muslim families as well, though the majority of them were in Hyderabad. It was quite different from Nellore or Madurai, and Gopalan enjoyed the change. He got a job at the King Edward Memorial Hospital.

He was a good doctor and earned a name and a good clientele. Everyone raved about the smart young doctor who had moved into town, and his lovely wife. Pankaja was happy. This was her home and family. Her very own place under the sun. The bleak clouds of misery and grief that had shadowed her childhood, began to fade. She blossomed in the warmth of Gopalan's affection and the admiration of his patients. He would come home for lunch around one and after serving him a deliciously cooked meal, she would sit with him on the swing, folding betel leaves to which she had applied *chunam* (lime), and handing them to him one by one.

He was very much in love with her and as he took each leaf, his eyes would twinkle and his fingers brushed against her cheek or breast. It was the most idyllic moment of the day for Pankaja, filled with the promise of the joys to come. The children played at their feet and they were a picture-perfect family.

He had bought a car and would take Pankaja and the children for a drive in the evening. He was proud of her beauty which drew admiring glances from passers-by and patients alike. Pankaja, who had finally escaped the misfortunes of the family of three widows, was happily married. She had children, she and her husband were prosperous and they led a fulfilling life. She was grateful that God had heard her prayers and had indeed been kind to her.

The fierce reformer and writer Veeresalingam Pantulu had begun to promote women's education and widow remarriage. Pankaja, who followed the news keenly, was delighted. For reasons close to her heart, Panthulu was a much-admired figure for her. She followed his ideas and his writing closely.

She had seen Pattamma's suffering as a young widow first hand. She had also watched her mother, who was wise and strong, suffer the terrible humiliation of widowhood. Her mother had initially refused to shave her head and continued to live in dignity in her own home. But when Pankaja fell seriously ill some years ago, her mother could not muster the courage to enter her in-laws' house with an unshaven head. She could not risk Pankaja being humiliated or insulted because her mother refused to conform to tradition. She sent for the barber and bowed her head. After her bath, she reached for an unbleached sari. When Pankaja, who was seriously ill, saw her mother thus disfigured, she sobbed more grievously than she had when her father had died. Mother and daughter clung to each other, weeping.

After a while, Rajamma said, 'Hush, daughter! It's only hair after all. This feels comfortable. I'm fine, child.'

18

It was a day like any other. Slightly windy and warm. The gate creaked open and a woman walked in. Standing in front of the verandah of Pankaja's house, the woman hesitated for a moment. The sound of Pankaja's rippling laughter and a glimpse of the good-looking doctor nuzzling his wife's cheek as he left the house, filled the woman with a strange fury. Her eyes filled with tears. How lucky Pankaja was! She looked away, her eyes filling with tears. Gopalan stepped out hurriedly. The woman tried to speak to him but he curtly informed her that he was late for work and asked her to speak to his wife. His car door slammed and the Morris Minor sped past the gate. Pankaja, who had stepped out to see him off, turned to the visitor with a smile.

'Amma! What can I do for you?' she asked.

'I came to meet the doctor. I am from Bezawada

(Vijayawada). Ram Mohan-garu sent me to meet him,' the woman, Bhagya said.

Pankaja looked at her inquiringly.

'I have passed my B.Ed. I am looking for a job,' Bhagya explained.

Pankaja noticed that Bhagya was not wearing a *bottu* (nose ring) and looked at her pityingly.

'Come in and sit down. He may be home for lunch if he finishes his rounds early. Otherwise, he will only come in the evening. Where are you staying?'

'At the government women's hostel.'

Pankaja offered her a chair on the front verandah. She sat at the edge of her seat. Pankaja gave her a glass of cool water from a mud pot and went about doing her chores. After she had cleared up the kitchen and put the children's toys away, she brought a pile of washed clothes in, placed them on the bench and began to fold them. When she was done, Pankaja turned to Bhagya, who had been observing her through the corner of her eye. Pankaja felt faintly uneasy for a minute. Then, setting aside her qualms, she asked her, 'How do you know Ram Mohan? Is he related to you? And when did you graduate?'

'Ram Mohan is related to my husband. I graduated last year.'

'Have you met Sister Subbalakshmi? I have always admired her and wanted to meet her...'

'Yes, I know her. But why does someone like you need to meet her? You have everything that any woman would wish for! A well-known husband, a lovely family and a beautiful home. Some people are truly blessed,' said Bhagya, barely hiding a trace of bitterness.

Pankaja felt a shiver run down her spine. It was as if an ill wind had blown in. Calming herself, she said, 'Well, that is God's will. I am sure you too will find good luck one day. You have worked very hard and suffered. That has its own rewards. Would you like some coffee?'

Bhagya shook her head and Pankaja resumed her duties. She liked to take a short nap in the afternoon, but she couldn't leave a strange woman alone in the house and go to sleep. She picked up the newspaper and began to skim through it. She did not make any further attempt at conversation. Bhagya turned away and kept gazing at the lime tree in the garden. Soon, it was four and the boys were home from school. They looked at the visitor for a second and rushed to hug their mother, talking excitedly and tossing their schoolbags in a corner. Pankaja drew them into the kitchen after they had washed their hands and feet, and set some biscuits and a tumbler of warm milk before them. They finished it hastily and then rushed off to play.

'Be careful! Come home early and start studying,'

Pankaja shouted out. She turned to Chudi who had followed them in and was drinking her milk. After Chudi was done, Pankaja loosened Chudi's plait and began to comb her hair. She reached for the string of jasmine she had kept in a basket on the table and pinned it on Chudi's hair. Chudi put on a fresh *bottu* and ran out to the garden. She was singing a melodious tune. Her music tutor would come in half an hour and teach her a new *varnam* (Carnatic music composition). Chudi had a clear, bell-like voice and her father loved to hear her sing.

It was time for her husband to come home. Pankaja set some water to boil for a fresh pot of coffee. She asked Bhagya whether she would like some buttermilk. Bhagya shook her head and Pankaja went about her work in the kitchen, making fresh vadas for her husband and preparing for the evening meal. She liked to finish her work in the kitchen by the time he arrived. That way, she would be free to sit and chat with him about the day's happenings as he sipped his coffee, watching the children play, and relaxing after his long day.

It was nearly dusk when Gopalan drove past the gate, which the children had left open for him. He entered briskly, smiling at Pankaja who had come out to the verandah to greet him. This was when he saw Bhagya through the corner of his eye. Irritable at the end of a long day, he snapped, 'Why are you here? Why didn't you come to the hospital?'

Pankaja interrupted him saying that she was not a patient but someone who had come to them looking for help. Controlling his irritation, he went in, had a bath and finished his coffee. He stretched his tired body for a few minutes. Leaning closer to Pankaja, he spoke to Bhagya impatiently.

'Yes? What do you want?'

Bhagya's eyes filled with tears as she told him why she had come. He asked her curtly to come to the hospital the next afternoon with her certificates and promised to do what he could to help her find a teaching job. She thanked him. Turning towards Pankaja, she smiled slightly. Pankaja was filled with pity for Bhagya and hoped her husband would help the poor woman in her job search. She felt the touch of Gopalan's hand on her shoulder and turned eagerly towards him. Bhagya left the house quietly.

Pankaja was at the height of happiness. She had it all: a loving and successful husband, healthy children and a circle of admiring friends. What more could a person want! She performed pujas and celebrated all festivals with great zest. Their home sparkled with laughter, music and the excited chatter of children. The sun shone brightly on her world and she was sure that the light would never dim.

19

Bhagyalakshmi was a young woman from Vijayawada. Widowed as a girl, she had been put through college and trained as a teacher in Sister Subbalakshmi's school for widows, in Madras. After completing her training, she went to Secunderabad in search of a job. Her uncle who knew Gopalan sent her to him for help. Insecure, young and all by herself in a strange city, she looked up to the doctor and hoped that he would be a source of support. Her heart was filled with admiration for the successful and handsome doctor.

She was a fair, plain-looking, big-built woman who envied Pankaja's grace, intelligence and beauty. The doctor was charming and his patients adored him. His colleagues and the staff at the hospital had nothing but praise for him. Nobody harped on his weakness for women. Even the gossips kept quiet about it. Secure in his love and in her marriage, Pankaja too was untroubled by his weakness.

The next day, Bhagya dressed in a neat grey sari, her hair well-oiled and combed, appeared at the KEM Hospital clutching a brown paper envelope, which contained her certificates and a couple of testimonials. The doctor was busy and he asked her to leave the file with his nurse. She was too nervous to ask any questions so she handed over the file to the nurse and left. She came back in the next two days, but he was far too busy and so she couldn't meet him. The third day, she tried again and stood timidly at his office door. He raised his eyebrows, puzzled, and then remembered that this was the woman from Bezawada.

'Come in! I have been too busy to meet the school's headmistress but if you wait a little, I will try and contact her,' he said.

He sent a boy to the headmistress's house with a note. The boy relayed the message that she was at home and would be happy to meet the doctor. Telling the nurse to check on the patient in Ward 3, Gopalan went to fetch his car. Bhagya followed him and modestly got into the back seat. The headmistress welcomed him and giving Bhagya a look, stretched out her hand for the papers Bhagya had brought.

'So, what subjects can you teach?' she asked, glancing at the certificates.

Bhagya murmured that she could teach Maths,

Science and Telugu. She was not strong in English but could make an effort. Bhagya was too tense to sit down. Everything depended on this interview. She desperately needed the job. The headmistress said that she did not have a vacancy right then but Bhagya could come in and be a substitute for teachers who were on leave for a couple of months. As soon as there was a vacancy, she would try to add her to the regular staff.

'Actually, I am doing this only because the Doctor brought you here personally and recommended you,' she added curtly.

Bhagya asked if she could start the next day itself. When she was told that she could, she turned to Gopalan with a grateful look. He just cleared his throat and left abruptly. Crestfallen, she walked out by herself and took a bus back to the hostel. She had hoped to go back in the car with him, visit his home and give the news to his wife personally. That woman intrigued her and the strong bond between the couple aroused an indescribable feeling of envy and emptiness in her. Her own marriage had been drab and disappointing. Her husband had died of typhoid, depriving her of even that dull security.

The next day, when she went to the school, she wore a slightly brighter silk, powdered her face and placed a small black dot on her forehead. It was barely noticeable but it broke the monotony of her bare forehead. Her nostril was bare but she wore a pair of modest earrings. She took care to look neat without attracting any undue attention. She had a prominent bosom so she wore a firm bodice under her blouse so that her breasts would not attract vulgar looks.

Bhagya was intelligent enough to know she had to play her cards very carefully to get what suddenly appeared to be a desirable goal. She made it a point to visit the doctor in the hospital every week under the pretext of thanking him and reporting on her progress. Her gratitude and ardent admiration slowly earned Gopalan's attention. Evidently, he would not have minded an encounter or two with her.

But Bhagya was shrewd. She was looking for respectability and stability. She was not going to give in easily to a one-night stand or a shoddy affair on the side. She was determined to displace the elegant Pankaja whose poise and charm disturbed her deeply. Her degree seemed worthless before Pankaja's knowledge and awareness of current affairs.

Pankaja was blissfully unaware of these churnings. She encouraged Bhagya by saying that with luck she would soon find a suitable match. She was sure to marry again and find some comfort in life. The memory of her sister's widowhood tore at Pankaja's heart. She looked out among their acquaintances for a suitable match for Bhagya. Little did she know that Bhagya had found her match. And she had quietly set a match to Pankaja's future.

20

One afternoon, Bhagya arrived at Pankaja's house. Glad to see her, Pankaja set aside the book she was reading and welcomed her with a warm smile. Bhagya said that since she had no class that day, she had thought it would be a good idea to come visiting. She was eager to chat with Pankaja and spend time with her. 'Bhagya! Make yourself comfortable. Tell me all about yourself,' Pankaja said, never doubting her visitor's intentions.

Bhagya was happy to share. She told her that her father had died of liver disease. She had four siblings: three brothers and a sister. The sister was settled in a village near Vijayawada. Her husband was a farmer and she had three children.

'My story is the worst,' Bhagya sighed. 'I was married off at fourteen and my husband died of typhoid when I was fifteen. One year of married bliss was all there was.

Fortunately, Ram Mohan Uncle talked to my mother and sent me off to Madras. Otherwise, I would have been rotting in Bezawada. After I passed my exams and began to feel human again, I came to Secunderabad hoping to find a job. Thanks to Doctor-garu's kindness, I have a job now.'

'What about your hostel? Is it comfortable?'

Bhagya sighed, then sneered. 'Yes, four walls and two meals mean comfort, I suppose. The warden is strict and treats us as if we are thieves living off government charity. Anyway, she is probably right. Who respects a woman without a family and a home of her own?'

Bhagya wiped her eyes which were filled with tears. Pankaja looked at her sympathetically.

'I feel so nervous,' Bhagya said. 'The government officers send for a girl whenever they want. And the warden sees to it that the girl they ask for is sent to them. In the evenings, young men hang around the gate and sometimes the gatekeeper will let a girl slip out for a couple of hours. He gets his money that way.'

Pankaja was shocked. This was a government institution set up to help single women who were working in the city and needed a safe place to stay. They had left their homes in smaller towns and villages and come to the city to earn a living. But people looked down on women who had to work for their living or to support their families. The courage and determination of these working women did not count. A woman who was homeless and sought shelter even if she paid for it herself was considered cheap, available.

Unfortunately, even the wardens, who were responsible for their safety and dignity, abused and humiliated them. It was ironic that any family, however poor, provided more dignity than singledom. If even the officers misbehaved with them and exploited them, what hope was there for women to work and grow? Why was it that the government that set up these hostels to shelter single women did not discipline and punish the officers who exploited the very people they were supposed to keep safe?

Even the institutional ones that were set up by the YWCA or the Andhra Mahila Sabha did not take any steps to train their staff to respect and protect the dignity of these women. She had heard complaints from trainee nurses and typists about how the husbands and sons of the wardens misbehaved. It was a shame that the family was the only shelter recognised as the proper one for a woman who was not married or who had lost her husband. And even within the family, she had seen enough examples of what was done to women who were single.

She shook her head in despair, 'This is terrible.

Would you like to come and stay here for a few days, till your mother comes and you find a house? There is a spare room and it is no inconvenience for a week or two. I will ask my husband.'

Bhagya's eyes lit up. She moved in without wasting any time. Pankaja, however, was soon troubled by the fact that every time she sat down with Gopalan to have a chat, Bhagya would walk into the room with some excuse, wrecking the intimacy of the moment. She also began to set the time of her going to school so that it would coincide with Gopalan's departure in the mornings. Inevitably, he offered her a lift. And soon, she moved to the front seat from the back. Within a week, she started to return with him at the end of the workday, after looping around the hospital.

Pankaja was a little uneasy but dismissed these feelings as unworthy of her. She was a poor widow's daughter after all who was not in the habit of picking fights. Unaware of Bhagya's intentions, Pankaja gave her hope. She reassured Bhagya about the future and told her not to worry. Love and marriage would be hers again and she would find comfort in life. But Bhagya had meanwhile begun to visit the doctor at the hospital, pouring out her woes and drinking in his sympathy. And Gopalan began to pity her vulnerability. Always attracted to women, he felt strong and protective when he was with Bhagya. Coming from a family of strong women who stood up to fate, this damsel in distress evoked pity in him. He felt strong, powerful and manly in the face of her helplessness. The passion that Pankaja's strength of character evoked, melted and flowed towards this soft, jelly-like mass of flesh with limpid, pleading eyes.

Besides, times were changing. A friend of his called Ram Mohan had just married an educated widow even though he had a wife and four children. Ram's wife was a helpless, simple soul who accepted her position without protest. She bore the countless humiliations heaped on her patiently. Her children suffered deeply.

Bhagya was calculating. As soon as she realised that he was flattered by her unconcealed admiration, she was determined to settle only for marriage. She was not going to cave in and be satisfied with an affair on the side. Her mother, an old, cunning hag, arrived promptly and tutored her on how to play on his weakness and get what she desired.

21

One day, Pankaja sat down beside Gopalan on the swing, gently stroking his shoulder, which was always sore. She said, 'Your friend, chemist Chari, who lost his wife last year, is a nice man. Why don't you sound him out on marrying Bhagya? He has a couple of young daughters so it will be good for them as well. And she will be happy with a gentle soul like Chari. It will be a good deed for you to perform.'

'Chari? He is a fool. Bhagya is too good for him!'

'He is no fool. Just a simple and decent man. For a widow to get a decent man is not easy. And, she has no wealth either. If you persuade him, you would have done a truly good deed.'

'Why can't I do the good deed by marrying her myself? As a matter of fact, I have been thinking about it. What do you say?'

Shocked, she looked at him to see if he was joking. He was serious.

Pankaja's head reeled. Darkness swirled around her. Maybe this was why old aunts said, 'Never say, *aiyyo*, *paavam* (poor thing)! In six months the same *paavam* will come straight back to hit you!'

Seeing how pale she looked, Gopalan grew anxious and checked her pulse. Pulling her hand away, she said, 'It's nothing. Probably morning sickness. My period is delayed.'

Gopalan was delighted but she pulled away saying that she was tired. She decided that she must get rid of this pregnancy. Immediately. Without his knowledge.

She met the lady doctor at the hospital the next day and asked for some pills. She pretended the pills were for her poor maid.

'Why did you come, Amma? I would have sent it with Sir.'

'There is no need to trouble him over these small things. You know how men are. He may send her away and she would end up jobless.'

They shared a good laugh. Pankaja picked up the pills, thanked the doctor for her help and headed home.

She had spent countless hours worrying about this young woman and wondering how to help her. And the woman had been busily digging Pankaja's grave! Naive Pankaja had never suspected the root of Bhagya's discontent. It only dawned on her on that terrible day when Gopalan had snapped back at her and her glasshouse came crashing down, the shards reflecting memories of Pondavakkam and Madras. How could she have been so blind! So trusting!

Bigamy had not been prohibited by law yet. So, quite a few men who were well off had begun to marry educated widows as a status symbol, keeping their first wives at home as glorified mothers and housekeepers. It was as if a crop of educated widows, like a murder of crows, had descended on the city in search of jobs and husbands! The thought of having two wives, one educated and working, and the other to manage hearth and home, suddenly seemed very tempting and practical to men. Many women who were aware of these dangers were opposed to the law prohibiting bigamy. They knew that their husbands would simply divorce them to marry this new crop of educated widows who now infested the community.

Young bachelors were hesitant fearing the widows' misfortune might affect their lives. But married men, already protected by the power of their first wives' *mangalsutras* (wedding necklaces), had nothing to fear. If bigamy was prohibited, then they, the first wives, would be divorced, thus losing their status as wives in the household. It was a question of survival, their legal status, and their rights to property and position. They were not ignorant women but incredibly aware of the hazards of such reforms. It was a 'heads I win, tails you lose' situation. It was only when Bhagya entered her life and rejecting her help, made a bid instead for her husband that Pankaja grew truly bitter.

Is this what widow remarriage was all about? Destroying families and throwing wives into the abyss? Playing on the lust and stupidity of men and seeking respectability at the cost of traditionally wedded wives? Wives who had no refuge? Which family would take back a daughter whose husband was alive! Which hostel would give such women shelter? Who would provide for their children's needs? Who would even think of questioning the man's impartiality? Pankaja wondered how her sons would grow up in a place poisoned by distrust, envy and anger. She wished she could have sought out Pantulu and talked to him about these matters. Would he have had any answers for her?

Pattamma had been right. Periyar spoke of equality, not of social reform. He spoke of rights. The rights of women to marry or not to marry, and the right to choose a partner. Pankaja sat lost in thought, pondering the differences between Pantulu and Periyar, and realised that Periyar's position on women was the clearer one.

Hearing Gopalan's car turn past the gate, she stood up. Earlier, she used to wait for the car to swing into her sight so she could catch a glimpse of his dimpled smile. That delight had been replaced by the sight of Bhagya sitting beside him proudly as he drove in. She sighed. Now, she simply went to the kitchen and boiled the water for his coffee. It was only after he called out to her that she appeared with his coffee and snack.

'What is the matter? Do you have a headache? Why is your face so pale?' he asked anxiously. She just shrugged and turned away to attend to her chores. Gopalan was troubled. He had expected her to be upset by his decision to marry Bhagya but had no fear that he would lose her.

After all, where could she go? And besides, he still loved her passionately. Bhagya was just an add-on and being headstrong and stubborn, he could not tolerate the fact that Pankaja was withdrawn. He had imagined himself to be Vishnu with a willing consort on either side. His fame and success had gone to his head and obscured his vision totally. He was trapped between his ego and his need for Pankaja. She was a pillar of strength and he relied on her. He would force her to accept his decision. He was not prepared to lose her so easily.

22

Gopalan was in a hurry to free himself of his responsibilities so he found a match for Chudi, who was thirteen and still in school. He wanted his daughter to be settled before he married again. Pankaja protested. She told him that he did not have the capacity to manage two wives, and that Chudi should continue with her schooling. Always brutal when opposed, he began to thrash Pankaja violently and regularly. He loved his wife but he hated her courage and independence. The fact that she would not consent to his second marriage made him even more violent than usual.

Pankaja walked around with bruises and welts all over her arms and back, and when the children or servants asked her what was wrong, she just covered the bruises with her sari and said that she had hurt herself. The more obstinate she was, the more enraged and violent he grew.

Chudi was married off against Pankaja's will. And within six months, Gopalan married Bhagya. When friends and family protested, he threatened to pour kerosene over himself and set fire to himself. His friends relented. They pleaded with Pankaja who shrugged and turned a deaf ear. They suggested that she should adjust. Adjust? She had adjusted all her life. To her father's illness. Her sister's widowhood. Her mother's sorrow. That huge cacophonous Kandala family and their eccentricities. And when she had, at last, found some hard-earned peace, she was expected to adjust to this viper that had slithered into her home and poisoned her life?

No, she was done adjusting. She tossed her head back and turned away. She would not compromise. She was willing to pay the price for her pride and self-respect. She thought of Pattamma longingly. Her sister would have been a pillar of support at this terrible time. Wiping the tears that were streaming down her cheeks, she reached for a sheet of paper and began to write to Pattamma.

23

Pankaja was determined. She refused to live under the same roof as the other woman and moved with her children to a small outhouse in a friend's bungalow. Gopalan used to visit her there as well. He could not live without her. But there was a tight knot of anger in Pankaja's heart. An icy contempt that this was not the man she had thought him to be. When he wanted a meal, she served him politely, with a tinge of pity. When he wanted to sleep with her, she avoided him. He belted her in his anger at being denied. Besides, oddly enough, he still loved her and could not live without her. He just needed to cut her down to size. She was well informed, frank and spoke to him without any fear. This triggered his temper.

Bhagya continued teaching at the Keyes High School for girls. She bore him three children in quick succession. But her charm soon faded. She was insipid compared to the lean, spare strength that marked Pankaja. He began to visit Pankaja in the outhouse more frequently. When his visits grew too frequent Pankaja shifted to Nellore to the family house so that she was out of reach. She felt there could be no greater shame than bearing his children along with her step wife.

Her father-in-law had died a couple of years ago and her mother-in-law and Singaramma lived in the family house. When Pankaja moved to Nellore, she comforted herself that there would be no strife or violence in her life. She could just make ends meet and live peacefully, making sure that her sons studied and had a home that was free of conflict. She did not want them to suffer the toxic effects of their father's behaviour. It was left to her to provide them with a peaceful and safe home where they could thrive.

But soon enough she realised that peace was just a dream. Sampath, her brother-in-law, who lived next door was warm and welcoming in the first few weeks. One night, she heard a knock on the door. Startled, she listened carefully. Again, that knock, light but insistent. She stuffed a pillow against her head and tried to go back to sleep. But sleep eluded her and her eyes stayed open.

Why was he knocking at midnight? That door was always locked and was never used by the family. Any exchange of words with her was only at the front door or in the backyard near the well. And these were purely about transactional or property matters. Even Sampath's wife Kamala hardly spoke to her. A wary and puzzled Pankaja spent a sleepless night.

The next morning, Sampath stopped at her front door on his way to his clinic. He smiled as his brow crinkled into the deep line that cut across it. The fold gave him a villainous look. She looked at him questioningly.

He said, 'Pankaja, you are still young. Don't waste your time thinking of that stupid brother of mine. As long as I am here, I will protect you from all harm. I will look after your sons and see that there are no more children. My brother was a fool to have thrown away a pearl of such great value. I know your worth. Don't lock the door at night. Just humour me.'

A wave of nausea swept over Pankaja. Was this what it meant to have left your husband? That you were available to any man who fancied you? She shook in rage and clenched her teeth. Then, drawing a deep breath, she said in a calm voice, 'I don't need your help. Keep your distance from me. And your self-respect.'

Scowling in anger, he left. Pankaja realised that it was not easy to be a single woman and live independently.

She drew Singaramma near and kept her beside her. She tolerated Singaramma's complaints and her idiosyncrasies so that there was no whisper of gossip. She knew she must be radiant and pure when Gopalan came back to her. As he was sure to do one day.

Among her two sons, Seshadri, the elder one, studied hard. He was a good student, but Pankaja placed all her hopes on Ramji, the second son. The eldest had been his grandfather's pet and was far too independent and distant towards her. She wanted Ramji, her pet, to become a doctor. She dreamt of the day he would garner more fame and fortune than his father. He would be her revenge on her faithless husband! But women propose and the goddess disposes...

Slim, tall, fair and good-looking, Ramji had no great interest in his studies. He loved to play cricket and from the time he was fifteen most of the upper-caste housewives in town, bored with their husbands who were busy mounting servant maids and street vendors, decided that he was a luscious pastime to compensate for their potbellied and coarse husbands. They plied him with sweets and snacks and gifted him gold rings and chains. Ramji accepted these from them indifferently and being young and hot-blooded, enjoyed the interludes. He was signalled at as he was passing by, dragged into the houses and smothered by sweating, desirous female flesh.

He enjoyed the sex and was proud of his power to perform at will. Oddly enough it did not make him cruel or lusty. No predator, he was more of a willing toy. His good will, humour and affectionate manner remained unspoilt. Pankaja guessed what was going on but was powerless to take it up with him directly. What could she say on such matters after all? This would have been a father's duty and there was no hope of his father setting him right. She sighed and gave up the dream of this son challenging his father.

Her eldest, Seshadri, had been his grandfather's pet. His father's conduct had turned him bitter. At heart, he resented his mother for not having managed to keep her husband by her side. He was bored, unhappy and resentful in her presence. Over six feet tall and solidly built, Seshadri joined the army's Madras Regiment. He did not mind the tough drills and the discipline, but the mental sterility of a soldier's life irked him. One day, they were being taught how to hurl bombs at a target. He pulled out the pin and paused. The commanding officer yelled at him to throw the bomb before it exploded.

Something flickered in Seshadri's mind and placing the bomb in his commanding officer's hand, he said, 'Hold it, you fool!' and ran away. He was far away when the bomb that the officer had hastily thrown into the distance, exploded. He knew that if he was caught now, he would be tried and punished. He left town, found hiding places and wandered from place to place, wondering what to do next.

Basically, Seshadri was a youth who liked to use his mind. He read everything he could lay his hands on, stretching the muscles of his mind so that he was soon as well-informed as he was physically strong. The 40s was a time when the younger generation, fuelled by dreams and the vision of a free future, were looking for solutions. Some joined the Congress Party and threw themselves into the freedom struggle wholeheartedly. Seshadri joined the Communist Party. Soon, the Party was banned and he went underground. All the months he was away from home, Pankaja would call some passerby from the street to her home and feed him a full meal before she ate. She hoped that some mother somewhere would feed her son a handful of rice.

Seshadri was found and arrested soon. While he was being taken by train to Vellore jail, the train halted at a small station. Rising as if to stretch, he leapt out of the door of the train just as it started moving again. The guards had been caught napping and could easily have shot him dead if only they had been alert. Pankaja sighed when she heard the news and continued to feed a wayfarer every night, hoping against hope her son would stay safe.

24

Life went on smoothly in a manner of speaking. Pankaja focused on her family and the fields they owned. Her preoccupation with the freedom struggle also helped her to put her marriage behind. One day, she received a telegram from Secunderabad. Her husband had suffered a heart attack and was in the hospital. She suffered greatly when she heard the news. The thing she valued most in life was her marital status. After living in a house of three widows and hearing the insults that her widowed sisters-in-law had faced, she had prayed she would never be widowed. Bhagya's desperation to grab another woman's husband to escape widowhood too had affected her deeply.

She hoped that the power of her *mangalsutra* would protect her husband and save him wherever he may be. He must live and be well and she should remain and die a *sumangali* with a smear of turmeric and some flowers… She had to go and see him now that he was hospitalised. She was troubled at the thought of going to Secunderabad, but she was told he had asked for her. Even though she wanted to visit, she could not stay under that woman's roof even for a single night. So, she decided to go and stay in Chudi's in-laws' house for two nights. Old friends flocked there to see her and Chudi's mother-in-law was irritated by the crowd flooding the house.

Pankaja's hospital visit was embarrassing. He looked pitiful, lying on the bed looking at her pleadingly, and it wrung her heart but she was not going to give in to emotion in Bhagya's presence. Bhagya, red-eyed and teary, watched them like a hawk and did not leave the room even for a moment. She inserted herself between the other visitors and Pankaja. The visitors clustered around Pankaja out of affection and respect for her. Bhagya grew anxious and insecure. What was that appealing look Gopalan threw at Pankaja? She knew that he loved her and regretted this marriage. He had not expected Pankaja to leave him. What if Pankaja decided to move back into their house? What if Gopalan asked her to do so now that he was sick?

The whole world seemed to be conspiring against her. Just a few days ago. Gopalan's sister Rukmani had come to see him. Sitting by his side, she said, 'Why did you bring this on yourself? Pankaja was so perfect for you. You were such a good match. Why did you throw it all away and marry this woman and saddle yourself with this fate, my dear brother?'

Bhagya overheard this and passed a note to her husband saying that he should ask his sister to leave immediately. Gopalan reluctantly asked his sister to leave. She did not protest or make a scene, but she gave Bhagya a contemptuous look that made her shudder.

Bhagya was nervous. If something happened to him, she would be blamed. After all, she had already been widowed once. She lacked the purity and power of a chaste wife that could protect her husband and keep him safe. She had three growing children now and fear seized her. Pankaja, with her impeccable dignity, left on the third day while tears streamed down her broken husband's eyes. Eventually, he did recover and go home. However, he was reduced to a mere shell of his former self. His practice shrank and he had to retire from the hospital. The famous, successful doctor Bhagya had desired and married, crumbled before her eyes. The only thing that remained intact was his terrible fury and violence.

The circle was complete.

Sitting by herself on a stone bench in the garden, Bhagya looked back at how it had all begun. Suddenly, the memory of Gopalan's mother's voice floated into her mind. Her mother-in-law had been furious and she had cursed Bhagya's mother.

'You have ruined my son's life, you wretched whore! Do you think your sons will prosper? Mark my words! My curses will haunt you. You will live to regret this day,' she had prophesied.

Bhagya's mother had pushed her spectacles up the bridge of her nose and chuckled, unperturbed. She and her daughter had got what they wanted. What could these mere words do?

Fate, however, is ironic. And very difficult for mortals to predict.

Bhagya had three brothers. The eldest, Ramayya, was a Major in the army, and one day, he had been shot dead by an angry *jawan* (soldier).

The second, Madhu, was a student who had joined the Communist Party. He was intelligent, well-read and charming. One day, he swallowed some poison and was found dead in his room. They said that he had been suffering from depression.

The third, Kuppuswamy, was a simple fellow who had married rather late in life. One September, it was raining relentlessly. Thunder and lightning pounded the earth. He was travelling with his wife and two children to Madras for a wedding. The train derailed on a bridge and fell into a flooded rivulet near Jangaon station. His whole family had been wiped out along with hundreds of others in one of the worst train accidents in southern India. Not even their bodies were found.

Did curses come true then? Did angry mothers have the power to curse you and wreck your life? Had her mother's need for Bhagya's security brought about the violent deaths of all three of her brothers? Bhagya was overcome by sadness. Maybe Gopalan's mother's words had not been just words after all. The curses had worked. Shuddering, she drew her sari tightly across her shoulders and stared into the distance with teary eyes.

25

Kandala Rajamannar had five children: two sons and three daughters. The second son, Sampath, had been given away in adoption to a childless cousin. The elder son was Gopal. Rajamannar had two widowed daughters, Kuppamma and Singaram. The other daughter, Rukmani, was well-married and settled. She lived in Madurai. They were fairly prosperous.

Rukmani had three daughters and one son. The son, Jagannathan, was intelligent but utterly lazy and spoilt. As an only son, he felt no pressure or need to achieve anything. No interest in working hard or proving himself. The youngest child, a son born to his parents after three daughters, he got by on charm alone. He barely managed to get through college. His sisters, on the other hand, worked hard, got their degrees and were all married off to high-ranking officials. Jagannathan drifted around for a bit looking for a job and went back to Nellore. He was at home there and he felt it would be easier for him to find work. He got a job as a clerk in a private firm and was quite content.

Jagan was not at all like his strict father, who was a man of principles. He resembled the men in his maternal family who clutched at every girl within reach. Whether it was a cousin, a neighbour or a servant, it mattered little to them. Female flesh like, fresh air and water, was meant for their enjoyment alone. Only sisters-in-law were considered taboo.

One day, Jagan came across a smart young girl at the post office. She caught his attention immediately. Krupa was a teacher in the local school. She was bronzed and slender, with a thick, wavy plait and curls that spilled on to her forehead. Jagan struck up a conversation with her and she was drawn to his charm, good looks and sparkling sense of humour. He was also well-read and an interesting conversationalist.

They began to meet regularly on her way home from work and would stop for a cup of tea at the tea shop at the end of the day. Jagan, who was a smooth talker, kept her entertained, while carefully avoiding the quizzical look of the tea shop owner. Sometimes, they went to the banks of the Pennar to sit there and watch the river flowing on as Jagan regaled her with his colourful stories.

For Krupa, who had no such entertaining friends, this was a pleasure. She was well-read, industrious and good at her work, but Jagan brought a hitherto unknown dimension into her life that lifted her out of the monotonous daily routine. His humour, anecdotes and obvious admiration made her heart beat faster. One evening, she succumbed to his charms and found herself in his arms. Not long after, Krupa had missed a period. Jagan reassured her glibly. His chief asset was his utter lack of principles. He was confident that he could wriggle out of the situation in good time and leave for Madras without taking on any responsibilities.

One day, one of her cousins caught sight of her laughing with him and cornered him. She was a Mala and in the 50s, the Malas in Nellore were a well-organised and militant lot. Jagannathan, who had simply been looking for some fun, found himself cornered one day by a group of youths at a lonely spot. They were dead serious unlike him.

'Hey! *Bapana Lanzhakoduka* (Brahmin whoreson)! Do you think you can get away with ruining one of our girls?' They confronted him angrily.

Jagannathan was shocked at the threat of violence in their tone. He had not bargained for this at all.

He thought desperately for a way to escape the situation. Marrying a Mala girl? Was that his only option to get out of this alive?

'No! No! I want to marry her!' he blurted out in sheer fright.

The Mala men felt jubilant at pinning him down and went straight to the Communist Party Office. They spoke to the leaders who were only too happy for a chance to prove their revolutionary mettle. The Party arranged a social marriage in the Town Hall and it was the talk of the town. Banners were put up and pamphlets distributed. The only son of one of the leading Brahmin families marrying a Mala girl! Jagan the never-do-well had become a hero after boxing himself into a corner. There was nothing heroic about him, but he put on a brave face and swaggered around. At the wedding, many speeches were given. Jagan's courage and his progressive character were praised by one speaker after the other. The youth were jubilant.

Soon, the speeches ended. Garlands were exchanged, slogans raised and the knot was tied. A Gordian knot! Tea and biscuits were served and there was laughing and backslapping among the youth. The Party leaders felt taller and soon the event was over. The bride and groom, clutching their garlands, quietly hurried away to her house. While the youth were chattering happily, there was an uneasy quiet among the caste elders in the Mala quarters.

What price would they have to pay for this? They

had seen too much humiliation and contempt to grow so jubilant. The future remained to be seen. Was this any victory at all? What good could come of this so-called marriage? Marriage was a community event. A union of families. A strengthening of the bonds in the community. They had seen too much humiliation and contempt in their lives to grow jubilant. The future remained to be seen. It was not such a simple task to take on the Brahmins since they had the support of all the other castes. And they controlled the big Gods: the powerful ones. The Pochammas and Mallamas might protect them from the pox or a fever but the powerful Gods controlled everything that mattered: the harvest, the rain, flood and famine.

And it was the Brahmins alone who could speak to these mighty male Gods. But the young hotbloods, now educated, full of ideas of equality, impatient with injustice and clamouring for change, saw this marriage as an assertion of their right to dignity and justice. How could a few letters change the course of fate? The elders shook their heads gravely and waited for what was to come.

26

Pankaja sighed and groaned as she turned over. 'He is not evil,' she stammered incoherently. Just stupid. Don't punish him. Teach him a lesson but spare him. Spare him…' She woke up with a start, sweating profusely. She looked around in a daze. Slowly, the pain began to twist her gut. She pressed the old pillow against her aching belly and slid into sleep. And began to dream…

27

The Brahmin quarter reeled in shock and horror. There was total silence. The usual chants of holy verses were not to be heard. The smell of incense did not linger in the ominous, dark silence. Even the fires were not lit in many of the houses. The shame, the sheer horror of it, made them all retreat into the dark. The only son from one of the leading Brahmin families. A groom to whom they would have gladly offered a lovely, sparkling daughter of theirs, with jewels and dowry in tow, as soon as he got a job. So many families had waited patiently for this moment. Nursing so many hopes in their hearts. And now this…What a state of affairs! Govinda! Govinda!

Jagan's father, Parthasarathy, who was in Madurai, heard the news. Covering his face with a towel, he flung himself face down on his cot. His mother sobbed grievously, hitting her head against the wall in a corner.

After a considerable while, Parthasarathy went in and had a bath with his clothes on as one would after a funeral. His wife sobbed, murmuring, 'no…no.' He flung his towel at her. She too had a bath while chanting, 'Govinda, Govinda! Save him.'

Jagan's name was never mentioned in the house thereafter. The daughters came and delivered children and left. They visited for festive occasions, which were sombre and joyless. Finally, Penda put up a picture of her brother on the wall of the front room. Her mother stuck a flower under the frame. Jagan was now safely consigned to the realm of the dead.

One day, Pankaja, who was visiting the Nellore house, was sitting on the front *piyal* (porch) of their Stonehousepet home. She lived in Madras with her sister now and had come to check on the harvest. It was a summer evening. The shopkeepers' wives on the street had washed their faces with fragrant Mysore Sandalwood soap, heavily powdered their faces with Ponds talcum powder, applied heavy black kohl to their eyes, oiled, combed and plaited their hair, the older ones twisting it into a neat knot. They had drawn out string cots on the street in front of their homes. After placing the fragrant jasmine they had picked on the white sheets spread on the cots, they began to weave them into pretty strands. Small garlands were placed at the shrines inside their homes. They tucked in snippets, the daughters' hair and then carefully wound strands of flowers into their hair.

Fragrant and fresh, they waited for their husbands to return home from work. The coloured saris they wore during the day were discarded and they were all dressed in saris in varying shades of white. Some gleaming white, some yellowed with age or dirt but all of them freshly washed. Dark colours were for house work and cooking, but come evening, they would blossom forth in pure white to welcome their returning husbands.

The Brahmin wives also washed their faces and wore flowers, but did not bother to signal sexual attraction. They knew it would happen anyway, or not. They would never wear white, which for them, was the colour of widowhood. Their lives were colourless enough as it is.

Pankaja answered the greetings and questions that neighbours called out to her. A deaf-mute shoemaker called Pochaiah stopped to chat with her. He hooted and slapped his cheeks. He beat his head violently, pointing to the house behind her. He placed three fingers on his forehead to signal the Iyengar caste mark. Pankaja knew he was signalling about her sister-in-law's son.

Then, the man hooted and slapped his mouth and cheeks. He mimicked the act of a shoe being stitched. Then, he indicated a girl, the cobbler's daughter. And made the signs of marriage: *taali* and *bottu*. He began to beat himself on the head and slap his cheeks and signal that the whole town was talking. Pankaja, who knew about it already, was more amused at his eloquence than shocked.

Singaramma came out and shooed him away in rage. It was her sister's son who had made the whole town freeze in shock. Komtis and Brahmins were the main occupants of the street called Pappula Veedhi. This event was a slap in their faces, an unbearable disgrace. It was alright to sleep with a Mala woman, all of them did...But marriage! The men were furious while the women sat in shocked silence, watching with wide-eyed horror.

Jagan found married life easy enough in the first few months. Krupa worked as a teacher in a local school. She gave tuitions in the evenings to earn a little extra money. As her pupils were upper-caste children, she had to sit outside the house in the front yard to teach them. Unfortunately, after marriage, the number of pupils dwindled and so did her income. She was a good cook and she kept a clean and welcoming home. Their son was a bright child, dark skinned like his father but sturdy and strong-limbed like his mother.

Jagan grew quite comfortable with married life. He liked a drink or two in the evenings but since he never got drunk, his wife did not mind. But he was lazy and overconfident. Soon, he lost his job due to his negligence. And he did not try too hard to find another or cut down the cost of his drinks. It did not occur to him to help his wife with their child, share the housework with her, or fetch things from the market. He played with his son when he was in the mood but seldom took on the responsibility when the child needed to be minded. An only son in a family of daughters, he had been thoroughly spoilt.

As time passed, he realised that Krupa was fed up with his lifestyle and his attitude. She began to neglect him. Their squabbles grew noisy and often violent fights broke out between them. The situation at home became unbearable. There was nothing but conflict in their lives now. Jagan decided to move to Madras to earn a living, leaving his poor wife and child to fend for themselves.

Ramji, Pankaja's son, was working and living in Madras. His wife, mother and aunt Singaramma also lived there. Jagan moved in for a few days with them. Pankaja was generous and broadminded. Thanks to her reading habit and her interest in politics, she did not object to an outcast nephew taking shelter in their house. Singaramma, however, was outraged and would finish eating her meals early, as soon as they were cooked, so that the food she consumed would not be the tainted leftovers from a casteless rascal.

Jagan would sit on the stone bench in front of the house and entertain Pankajamma with tales of his wife and her intelligence. He always assumed he would get a job and bring her to Madras. One day, the song, '*Pyar kiya toh darna kya*' from *Mughal-e-Azam* was playing on the radio as he sat with Pankaja. Jagan kept time, happily humming along.

He said, 'Mami, listen! Do you hear that song?'

Pankaja said mockingly, 'Yes, you fool! She is going dar, dar, par, par and you think you are a hero?'

Jagan shut up. He was an entertaining man who liked to boast and pretend that things were fine even when everything was falling apart. He had not found a job. His wife was not going to relent unless he started earning steadily. Here, where he was treated as a member of the family and made to feel welcome, he was not troubled by any principles. When he was short of money, he did not hesitate to pilfer from Pankaja's purse, which was kept under her pillow. But Pankaja, who was large-hearted and generous felt a deep pity for him and simply ignored the petty thefts. And she did not permit Singaramma to insult him either.

Finally, Jagan who saw no hope of finding a job after he was thrown out of the one that Ramji had got him, realised that it was time to move on. He said he was going back to Nellore. He reached the Central Station and as he was hurrying towards the ticket booth, he bumped into his father who had come to Madras on some work. The father-son duo stared at each other and Jagan's eyes brimmed with tears. He fell at his father's feet in genuine remorse for the anguish he had caused a parent who had loved him all along. His father choked on his tears. Clearing his throat, he said, 'You will have to undergo a *prayaschittam* (purification) if you want to enter my house.'

Jagan nodded shamefacedly, and signalled his assent in silence.

The purification ceremony was held in Madurai. After several dips in the Vaigai and a sacred thread ceremony on its banks, Jagan was taken home. His father had decided to do a *godaanam* (donate a cow) for good measure. A dappled cow was garlanded, fresh *kumkum* applied to its forehead and the couple went around it thrice, prostrated before it, and collecting the urine that the animal passed plentifully, sprinkled it on Jagan's head and placed a few drops on his lips. The cow was then handed over to a waiting Brahmin. It mooed loudly and followed him as he tugged at the rope.

Jagan's mother, after performing a camphor *aarti* (ritual), tears flowing freely down her cheeks, took his hand and led him in. He sat with his head bowed while she plied him with fruits and milk and honey first. And then a silver tumbler of steaming hot coffee covered with foam was served. Jagan's eyes brimmed as he sipped the coffee. He was filled with remorse that he had wounded his parents so badly.

He resolved to become a son they would be proud of. He must make up for the suffering he had caused them. A few close relatives dropped in and he felt he was back in the warmth of his family circle. His sisters wrote to him as well to share their joy. He was at peace. Krupa and the child became a thing of the distant past and he settled down at a new job his father's influence got him.

He had a regular routine soon. Months passed and his days were free of tension. He seemed to have tided over his troubles. His mother was trying to find a poor Brahmin girl for him to marry. But it was not so easy. He had lost his caste and all the rituals in the world could not make up for the fact that he was just an ordinary man doing a mundane job. However, he felt secure in his father's home and at ease.

But peace is an illusory thing. One day, a letter from Krupa arrived. She informed him that she had found a government job and was due for a promotion. She had enclosed a picture of his son saying that the child was in school and doing well. She was planning to marry again. Since they had gone through a civil marriage and Krupa was a government employee, she needed a divorce. Jagan felt a piercing ache in his heart. Suddenly, memories of his wife and child came flooding in. Filled with remorse, he decided to pay a visit to his wife and son.

He booked a ticket and left town, saying he would be back in a week. From Central Station he took the Grand Trunk Express which would get him to Nellore. In four hours, he was at Nellore. He hopped on a bus and reached Krupa's office. She looked paler and thinner, but composed. She glanced at him briefly and told him to wait while she wound up some work. When she was done, they took a rickshaw to her house and found the boy playing outside. He had grown and was dark-skinned like Jagan but he had inherited his mother's sharp good looks. Krupa went to the kitchen, made some tea and took out some *murukkus* (crunchy snack) from a tin. She set them down on a plate and served the tea. Jagan hesitated for a minute before drinking the tea.

She looked at him scornfully and said, 'So, it's true! You've been purified. You Brahmin bastard! Why did you come here with your tail tucked in between your legs? Is your father going to welcome his grandson, conduct a thread ceremony and make a priest of him?'

Jagan squirmed at her contempt. But he was trapped. Since she was going to marry again, he knew there was no place for him in her life. And there was no way he could offer to look after his son. He just drank a couple of sips of tea and said dully that he was leaving. He stretched out his hand and tried to caress the child who shrank from his touch. He walked out into the street and turned towards the station. His legs felt leaden and his head was heavy. Taking the next passenger train, he got back to Madras. The jolting and creaking of the train numbed and comforted his tortured mind.

He thought with a hint of amusement that his life was like the passenger train he had boarded. He had dreamt of being a bullet train or an express but, he was destined to be a passenger, halting at every signal to allow the fast expresses to speed by. Well, that was his life. The only son of a wealthy father, he could have chosen any career he wanted. But he had drifted along, little expecting that soon life would pass him by.

He remembered his cousin Gopi who would simply sit on the station platform, watching the trains shunting past from morning to evening. Gopi was the son of his Uncle Chamappa, who had gone mad and spent his time learning black magic in burning ghats. Once a station master, he had lost his sanity after his wife's death. Gopi was slow and no one bothered to check whether he went to school or studied when he was a little boy. But Gopi woke up when he was about ten and began to take school seriously. He worked hard, passed his exams and gradually acquired a degree. After moving to Hyderabad, he got a job as a clerk at the Secretariat, married and settled down in the city.

Even stupid, slow Gopi had made something of his life and his father was only a station master. Uncle Chamappa had four sons and two daughters. The only good thing he had done as a parent was to get his daughters married off. His sons were left to their own devices. After he suffered a mental breakdown, he took to witchcraft and black magic briefly. But he had recovered gradually and led a somewhat normal life. His sons had managed to secure a decent living for themselves on their own. Jagan, the only son of a wealthy father with nothing to fear, had failed unlike them. He was secure and so he had drifted. He sighed heavily and tried hard to think things through. One thing was sure. He would have to give Krupa a divorce and that galled him. It was yet another admission of his failures in life.

He thought of taking the next train to Madurai but his heart was heavy as lead. He could not face his father in this state. Leaving Central Station, he turned into one of the streets that branched off the main road. Iyer's Brahmin Hotel was open. They served piping hot idlis and sambar on steel plates covered with a shred of banana leaf. He ordered two plates of idlis and ate hungrily because he had not had a meal since the previous afternoon. Comforted by the taste of the idlis and the piping hot, frothy coffee, he walked out.

A few minutes later, a familiar smell assaulted his nostrils. He looked up at the Military Hotel. The aroma of omelettes, beef curry and parottas wafted out from there. This was a once-familiar smell. He remembered his cousin Seshadri telling him the story of the Military Hotels. When his cousin was in the Madras Regiment, the soldiers who were untouchables used to go to the Brahmin hotels. There, they had to stand outside on the street and were served food on leaves. A separate set of glasses, reserved for them, stood on a bench and tea or water would be poured into them from a proper height.

The British officers who observed this were incensed at the Queen's army being treated with such indignity. But no threats or requests could budge the iron wall of the twice born. Frustrated, they decided that the only way to protect the dignity of the Queen's army was to give a few lower-caste merchants funds to run hotels, which would serve the soldiers of the British army good food and seat them indoors with dignity. Once the Brahmin label was gone, it was logical to serve beef curry and dry fish with dosas or rice water. These were the favoured food items of the working castes.

Jagan, who had actually relished this food some years ago, found that the smell wafting out of the hotel made him shudder. He walked faster and turned towards the beach. Walking through Triplicane, he passed the Parthasarathy temple where the bells were chiming, reminding him of his duty. The hoarse chanting of mantras hammered at his temples and seemed to be calling him to account. His father's voice, gruff but caring, seemed to draw him back to his roots.

He got to the beach and walking across the sand, reached the edge of the water. He sat there for a long time, lost in thought. He brooded about the past and about what the future held. But the ocean did not provide any answers. Going back to Madurai was a frightening prospect. He left the beach and wandered around the streets. When he spotted a telephone in a small grocery shop, he pulled out a little diary from his pocket and dialled a number.

He realised that his cousin Ramji was at work. A

colleague of Ramji's shouted out that there was a call for him from Jagan. Ramji swore angrily and told his colleague to get rid of Jagan by telling him that he was busy. Jagan heard this and his heart sank. The one family member who had not judged him or rejected him had also washed his hands off him. A saddened Jagan walked around restlessly for a few more hours. Suddenly, he had a flash of insight.

Madras was overrun by rats at the time and rat poison was freely available. Stopping at a pesticide shop, he bought a packet of rat poison. Tucking the packet into his bag, he walked on. It was growing dark; he felt neither hunger nor thirst. Just an immense weariness. From a radio in a small shop, the notes of a favourite song of his drifted his way.

Nandadathaye ninaithirundhal amaidhi yengum illai
Ninaithadhellam nadandhuvithal daivamethumillai!
(Where is the comfort in dwelling on the past?
If everything went exactly as planned
Where is the need for a God?)

So true! His eyes prickled with bitter tears. A few moments of innocent fun and his life had spun out of control. Was he evil or wicked? Had he ever intentionally hurt anyone? He had married Krupa when her people demanded it. She had been wearied of him and his inability to hold a steady job. His father had taken him back in the end. The only son whom he needed to perform his last rites! And he had patiently gone through the purification rites and adjusted to a sober life. What more could he have done?

He sat there for a long time in silence. And then all his troubles vanished in a flash. He knew exactly what he had to do. He bought a small bottle of arrack as the sky darkened. Carrying it, he settled down on an empty bench and carefully emptied the rat poison into the arrack. Then, he briskly walked towards Fort St. George, his mind made up.

28

It was around noon when Jagan's father received a call from the Madras Police saying that his son had been found dead in front of Fort. St. George. He seemed to have died around midnight. His father got dressed in a daze and he told his wife that he was going to Madras to claim the body of their only son and perform the last rites.

When he reached the mortuary, he was stunned to see a young woman there accompanied by a group of rough youths. The police inspector said that she had come to claim the body of her husband. As his wife, she had priority. Jagan's father tried to explain that his son had recanted and returned home. It was useless though. Nobody listened to him. He wept as he watched the young men load Jagran's body into a van and drive away. He stumbled down the street to the beach and bathed in the sea. And then, it was time for him to return home to his grieving wife. His daughters who had by now heard the news had arrived as well.

There was a deadly silence in the house. No weeping or wailing. Nothing but absolute quiet, broken by the sound of the shuffling footsteps of their neighbours and relatives.

This was the end of the long line of a respected family. Narayana, Narayana…

The van went hurtling down the highway. It was a hot day and the body, packed in a straw mat and covered with ice, had begun to smell. After an hour, Krupa, sickened by the smell, shifted to the car they had hired. Her heart was heavy with regret. She remembered the dreams she had nursed when she started meeting Jagan. He had left his job when he was unhappy with it and she had carried on day after day, working steadily till she earned a promotion. The child was growing up. He had not missed his father after the first year. She was proud of him and he was the one thing that kept her going.

She had been hoping to settle down again and now Jagan had ruined it all. A slow rage filled her. She would always be branded the woman who drove a man to his death. The stigma would be attached to her no matter how hard she tried to get rid of it or how well she did in life from now on. Nothing would change. The whispers, sidelong glances and jibes would continue.

She felt faint with the heat, and asking them to stop the car, drank a cold lime soda. The liquid swirled in her stomach as they went on. Her head was throbbing and she felt sick. In a minute, the car had to stop for her to step outside and throw up. Splashing some water on her face, she got into the car again. After what seemed like eternity, they reached Nellore.

Washing her face and feet, she went into the house and flung herself on a cot. Her child came in and touched her cheek. She asked him to go outside and play and covered her face with a pillow. In about an hour, one of the young men arrived to inform her that the body had been taken to the banks of the Pennar. They were putting up a tent and a platform and were going to place the body there, right next to the Ranganathaswamy temple.

'But that is the Brahmin quarter!' she said, shocked.

'Yes, we have to teach these bastards a lesson.'

For three days and nights in the sweltering heat, Jagan was propped up in the tent next to the temple wall. Covered with flowers and garlands, his corpse seemed to mock the grandeur of the deity inside.

Drums beat relentlessly night and day for three days. The youth roared, 'The Brahmin has become a Mala! The Brahmin bastard has become a Mala!' Their rage was palpable.

They kept shouting all day. Again and again.

The Brahmins living around the temple froze in horror. They locked their doors and did not leave, even to bathe in the Pennar. No fires were lit. No lamps shone. No mantras were chanted. The Brahmins simply fasted and trembled in fear and horror. At last, on the third day, the young men cremated him after giving a few speeches and dispersed in triumph. Heaving a sigh of relief, the Brahmins in the area resumed their rituals. It was several days before they could even talk about it and that too in whispers. The Mala youth felt they had scored a victory but, in fact, nothing had changed. Either in their lives or in that of the Brahmins.

In time, Jagan, who was dramatic and notorious in death as in life, was forgotten. And the Penner flowed on placidly. Its waters swirled, untouched by anger or arrogance. Lord Ranganatha, radiating a peace that belied the fury enacted outside his sanctum, gazed at the world of mortals calmly, his name and ornaments shining bright.

29

Pankaja woke up, startled. Her eyes were filled with tears. Murmuring, 'poor child, foolish boy,' she sighed. She pondered the difference between Kannamma and Jagan. Kannamma was a middle-aged woman who had left her family of five grown children to live with a Mala *maddaliga*. She lived openly, untouched by her family's sneers or caste contempt. The sense of shame was entirely the family's burden to carry. She roamed free of guilt and remorse. Was it that women in crisis were stronger than men? Once they had broken the shackles of the family and thrust fear and guilt aside to face the truth, were women truly free?

Wasn't Kannamma far stronger than Jagan, who was torn between desire and wealth and family? But the family elders thought that Jagan had been misguided and betrayed. They blamed his wife for seducing him and killing him. They could not see the trap that he was caught in. The comfort and security of the family had invisibly held him captive. That was like a poisonous web and when he had tried to escape, unfit to run, he had died. Taken his own life. Whereas Kannamma had left without looking back. There was no value or comfort in the family for her.

Without her music, she would have been trapped in a loveless marriage permanently. But her music, the fact that she could face the public and earn both money and applause, had set her free from that web. *A web of deceit*. And she lived with her head held high while her critics cowered in shame. She had openly exposed the fragility of wifely virtue.

Startled, Pankaja woke up. She shook those unseemly thoughts out of her head. But now, in retrospect, were they really unseemly? Had she herself not clung to her *pativrata* (pure) image though her husband married another woman, foolishly thinking that her fidelity and devotion would surely bring him back to her? She had never judged her sister Pattamma for the free life she had led, choosing her lovers as she pleased. Pattamma had been widowed and forsaken and still had a right to her life.

Why had she found it so impossible to choose a lover who would have ensured her comfort and status? Why had she clung so devoutly through her hardship and suffering to an errant husband, never losing faith in him, always expecting that he would see the truth, escape the clutches of the other woman and come back to her in the end?

Pankaja shook her head and wiped the tears with her *pallu*. This was no ordinary ache. It burrowed deep into her soul, dredging up sorrow after sorrow. Was there a medicine for her heartache? How did one cauterise the heart? With a red-hot iron ladle? She would have gladly suffered that heat to escape this torture. One memory following on the heels of another, she had no respite from the demons that tore at her heart.

Coming from a house of widows, her only desire had been to die a *sumangali*. Decked with a pinch of turmeric and *kumkum* and a few flowers. But God's will prevails...She had realised long ago that there were widows and widows. There were the ones who suffered and those who survived. The ones who survived, eloped if they were lucky or stubbornly lived lives of dignity like her sister Pattamma. Inspired by Periyar, she never bowed her head, and lived freely. Then there were the ones like Bhagya. They managed to get an education but lacked the strength or character to live alone or to find a single man who would be glad to marry them.

The problem was that single men were nervous about marrying a widow and courting the bad luck it might bring their way. On the other hand, there was a crop of married men with wives and children, who felt it was fashionable to have an educated English-speaking wife they could flaunt in public while keeping their first wife and children in the same house. Given the resentment of the first wife and the envy and insecurity of the second, the whole thing was doomed. The first wife's children suffered and survived great hardship. The men, besotted with the new wife as they would be with a concubine and ashamed to defend the first, did little to manage matters.

Pankaja had many questions she would have asked the famous social reformers of the time if she had an opportunity. Why didn't they teach these women real independence? Why didn't they instil self-respect in them? Why did they set out to seduce middle-aged married men? What was the use of an education that merely taught women letters without the basic pride and self-respect that they needed?

When the law prohibiting bigamy was to be passed. Large numbers of married women protested because they were afraid that they would be divorced and left without status or rights, and their children disinherited. Women were so badly off that they felt it was far better to slave away in a corner of their husband's house, swallowing the humiliation and holding the poison in their throats for the sake of their children. Neelakanta (the blue-throated one, Shiva) now. No longer Lakshmis. After all, what was the point of a *mangalsutra* that did not guarantee your place beside your husband?

Pankaja tossed and turned on her bed...Dreams of the past...Her life drifting back to her in scenes...She had resolved, after seeing him lie sick and broken in the hospital pleading for her forgiveness, that this was not the man she had married. She did not want to be one of a pair of bullocks dragging a shattered cart across the plains. He had made his choices, betrayed her love and lost her trust. She had given her youth and beauty and strength to this man. And he had cast it all aside without a second thought. He had never imagined that she could leave him, that she would leave him. Lord, what fools these men were! How arrogant! She had seen his weaknesses and his strengths and loved him in spite of his faults. Forgiven the odd encounter when they were together.

But this betrayal of the bond that held them together, the arrogance of assuming that she had no choice! She had sons to raise when he married Bhagya. Brazenly, he had married off her daughter who was still in school to free himself for this second marriage. He did not want people to say that he had not fulfilled his responsibilities. He had stopped the child's studies and insisted that she settle down with unseemly haste. But her sons were with her and Pankaja had vowed to raise them to be real men. Strong, principled and self-reliant. Never bowing their heads to authority. Never turning to her feckless husband for help. She had succeeded at it. That made her smile and gave her some comfort.

30

The Kandala family had a *sarpa dosha* (powerful limitation in one's natal chart) since one of the ancestors had killed a king cobra that entered the house. In penance, the cobra was worshipped every Naga Panchami, and the eldest child of every generation was always named Sesha. Seshadri, the eldest grandson in the male line, Pankaja's firstborn, was the apple of his grandfather's eye.

Pankaja's life slowly settled into a groove, but peace is short lived. Her father-in-law and mother-in-law died within a year of each other. Since her mother-in-law died first, Pankaja was spared the ordeal of watching her going through the rites of widowhood. And since she was the only married woman left in the family, she dressed and decorated her mother-in-law's body one last time, praying that she would be granted an auspicious death.

Seshadri had always resented his mother's independence. Pankaja could do little to dispel his resentment, though he was mature enough to be fully aware of the truth. He refused to engage with her; grunting, speaking only in monosyllables or generally grumbling about the food she served, or the weather, as if even that was her fault. Though he had witnessed his father's brutality and was agitated and heartbroken, he resented the resistance his mother had put up. He held her responsible for his father's behaviour and kept his distance from her. He believed that she could have saved the situation if she had given in to him or swallowed her pride. According to him, she had failed them. However, at another level, he was also deeply disturbed by his father's violence.

Perhaps, this had something to do with his grandfather's disappointment in his eldest son. But the deeply ingrained attitudes he had inherited would not let him stomach the fact that she was a discarded wife. Even if she had chosen to walk away, she was still the *vazhavetti*, the rejected wife. He brooded about it and missed no chance to heap blame on her. No one else in the family blamed her for what had happened. She was respected and loved by her sisters-in-law and her mother-in-law.

Fondly called Chellappa at home, Seshadri had lived

a checkered life filled with adventure. Six feet tall, sturdy and dark, he had a quirky sense of humour. His life had been eventful both in the army and in the Party. Admired by his friends, and spoilt and adored by his family, he was used to being the centre of attention everywhere with his strange stories and jokes.

He was also strong and tough, and given his army background and his genes, prone to violence when he got angry. Once, a Komti grain merchant, who was her neighbour, thought that since Pankaja was a single woman, he could encroach on some of her land located at the back of the house. He sent a few men to set up a fence in the backyard, grabbing a large stretch of her land. Alarmed, she wrote a postcard to Chellappa, who promptly arrived at Nellore. After throwing his bag into the hall, he strode to the neighbour's house.

The man was eating his afternoon meal when Chellappa swung at him and struck him on the jaw. Stunned by the sudden violence of the blow, which sent his dentures flying across the room, he cowered. Stooping and picking them up, Chellappa yelled, 'Here, put them on, you son of a whore!'

Giving the startled man a minute to put them on, Chellappa continued to pound him, asking whether he would ever dare to bother his mother who was a single woman again. Once his job was done, he strode out of the house and went off to visit some of his old Communist friends who lived on the other side of town. The injured man lodged a police complaint. The police came to Chellappa's house but he was nowhere to be seen. They asked around for him and left.

Chellappa came home late at night from his friends' place, ate the rice and brinjal fry that Pankaja served him and went to sleep. He simply shrugged when his mother told him that the police had come looking for him. He left the next day on the morning train to Madras, and that was the end of the affair.

Once, when he had gone underground, he had developed a slight swelling in his testicles. Panicking, he went to the Madras General Hospital and the doctor told him he needed a minor surgery. He was admitted to the general ward. The surgery was a simple procedure. On the second day, however, he was shocked to find the very police inspector who had tried to arrest him in the bed next to his. The man kept saying, 'You look very familiar. I'm sure I've met you before.' Chellappa, who had grown a huge moustache, quipped, 'It must have been in the Rogues Gallery. Where else!' But he slept with his face covered, and carefully giving the policeman a wide berth, he left the hospital on the third day, heaving a sigh of relief.

Soon, it was time for Pankaja's sons to go to college. She leased the fields to a tenant farmer and decided to move to Madras to live with her sister, Pattamma, who was ill and needed her help. Weary of his adventures, Chellappa decided it was time to settle down. He joined Madras Presidency College in his late 20s to get a Master's degree in political science. Since he was already well-read and politically mature, the degree was child's play, a mere formal qualification, which would help him to find a teaching job. The truth was that he knew far more than his teachers. And after his tough life in the army and then in the Party, he was delighted to savour the simple pleasures of college life.

A few months after he got his degree, Aunt Pattamma whom he admired and respected, asked him whether he had any marriage plans. He had just been selected as a lecturer in Anwar-ul-Uloom College, Hyderabad. Having had enough of a carefree life, he thought that domesticity might be worth a try. Pattamma put out the word and soon found a good match for him. Jayanthi, a working woman in her mid-twenties, slightly older than the usual brides on the market.

She was a graduate who had joined the Railways as a lower-division clerk. She used to commute every day by electric train from Tambaram to college and later to work. Jayanthi was tall, fair and statuesque with eyelashes that spread fanlike across her cheeks. It was pure luck that they found a good-looking, educated girl. A slight flaw in her horoscope had kept her single. Most eligible girls were snapped up in their teens. Long before they turned twenty. She was not preoccupied with her looks like most girls her age. Luckily, she did not need to care.

Her clear complexion, her dark, arching eyebrows and her long, curved lashes made her breathtakingly beautiful. She and Chellappa made a perfect pair; he was tall, dark and handsome; she, statuesque and fair with chiselled features. Pleased with the match, her family made all the arrangements. The evening before the wedding, there was a procession, the *jaanavasam*. The groom was taken to the temple for a ceremonial welcome and a formal engagement. Garlanded and dressed in a suit, Chellappa was seated in an open car with a small-town band playing cacophonous music.

He put up with it for about five minutes and then, having had enough, stood up and shouted, 'Stop playing!'

Surprised at the bridegroom's conduct and his authoritarian voice, the band stopped. After a few minutes, however, they resumed the music since they were paid to perform by the bride's party. Again, he stood up with a roar, and jumping out of the moving car, collected all the instruments from them and dumped them in the car. The poor bandsmen walked along in nervous silence. Pankaja was appalled at his behaviour. She was afraid the bride's father might think her son was mad and cancel the wedding. No such disaster happened and the marriage ceremony went off smoothly.

It had always been a joke among the younger ones of the Kandala family that the new Brahmin fad in the 50s was that most grooms' families demanded a band and a music concert. That was mandatory just like the bride's diamond earrings. A concert that no one bothered to listen to in the crush of greeting, eating and gossiping!

The poor singer, having been paid, would sing her quota of songs accompanied by a violin and a mridangam. She would leave after taking her fee. Pattamma, however, not only enjoyed the music but also respected the artist. She invariably sat in the first row, fanning herself and listening to the singer, refusing to engage in greetings and gossip. The musician would sing with renewed passion to this attentive audience. Before leaving, the musician usually came and greeted her, and touched her feet. She was a cultured lady after all.

The band, a status symbol, was a recent addition to the traditional trumpets and mridangams that were meant to drown out all the inauspicious sounds during the *muhurtam* (auspicious moment). While the traditional instruments were at least passable, the bands were cacophonous, loud and out of tune. And yet, they were in demand!

31

Early in their marriage, Chellappa and his wife suffered a tragedy. Jayanthi conceived within a year of their marriage. She was in her mid-twenties and the baby was a late preemie. She went back to Tambaram as was the custom for her delivery. Chellappa dropped a bomb on the whole family when he refused to go there for the *srimantham*. This ceremony, held in the seventh or eighth month with the husband and wife exchanging garlands and receiving gifts, was a public acknowledgement of paternity.

In the few cases when the groom refused to participate, it was when he suspected that the child was not his. Shock waves jolted Jayanthi's entire family, but he would not budge. So, the parents conducted the bangle-gifting and flower-weaving ceremony in the seventh month, swallowing their embarrassment at his stubbornness.

When the child was due, Jayanthi's mother, in simple ignorance, decided on a home birth for her daughter. It had not occurred to her that there may be complications. After Jayanthi was in labour for several hours, the midwife finally threw up her hands and said it was better to go to the hospital. What pain and torture poor Jayanthi suffered on that hour-long ride to the hospital with the child's head stuck halfway, she never ever spoke about! However, that suffering was briefly erased by the fact that the child, beautiful, big and perfect, did not utter a cry at birth. She took this to be a good sign. Her father named him Ashok: the one without sorrow. But his freedom from sorrow would soon become a source of suffering for everyone.

The child grew physically till he was four. But he never cried, crawled or spoke a word. The doctors found out that the trauma of his birth had gravely damaged his brain. The pitiable condition of her son brought immense grief and bitterness into Jayanthi's life. Chellappa never displayed his feelings though he was bitter, nor could he comprehend the guilt that Jayanthi, an educated woman, felt in submitting to her mother's disastrous decision about her delivery. Since finding child care for a severely challenged child with a working mother was impossible, the boy was left behind with the grandmother at Chingleput.

It never occurred to Jayanthi to quit work and devote herself to the care of her child. Her husband's financial instability did not offer her that luxury. Gradually, Jayanthi grew more and more bitter at her fate. She loved her child but was tortured by his disability and her own sense of failure. The understanding and acceptance of disability had not yet set in in the mid-twentieth century.

Ashok had just begun to stand up and take a few steps when he was almost four. He also made a few incoherent sounds. One day, his grandmother picked him up as usual when she went to milk their cow in the barn in the backyard. Setting him down beside her and thrusting her head against the cow's side, she began to milk her. When she was done, she turned around and found the child missing. Thinking that her nephew must have picked up the child, she carried the milk pail back into the house. But to her dismay, Ashok was nowhere to be seen. A search was launched and they began to look for him in earnest everywhere.

Had someone kidnapped Ashok because he was so beautiful? Child sacrifice was not uncommon in those days. There was no trace of him and two anxious days went by. Late in the evening on the second day, they dredged open the nearby well and fished out the body of the golden child. A child who had barely managed to stand up had crawled or walked all the way to the well, which was twenty yards away from the house. The irony and cruelty of that accident embittered Jayanthi and Chellappa. They cursed their fate and raged against the unfairness of it all.

'Maybe it was God's will! What a terrible fate.'

'Strange are the ways of God! His *maya*! This child who had just taken his first steps and who couldn't go anywhere without an adult's help walked by himself to the well?'

'This is destiny. He was not meant to be yours.'

And so people went on and on...

Words which could not comfort and were not meant to, hung in the air. Why are such clichés mouthed incessantly when there is a tragedy? Silence would have been more soothing than these platitudes for the grieving family.

~

Jayanthi, being a working woman, had never learnt to cook. She was used to being served good food at home since her mother was an excellent cook, but she was simply not interested in cooking. She churned out indifferent meals in her hurry to get to work, which her husband swallowed with much difficulty. For her, food was just there to assuage hunger. This caused problems between her and Chellappa at times, especially, at the start of their marriage.

She was also thrifty to the point of stinginess and deeply troubled by her husband's casual attitude to money. It had never once occurred to her that his family had not demanded the customary dowry or insisted on the quantity of jewellery she brought with her or enquired about her salary. These could be seen as signs of their superior character. A small-town girl essentially, she could not think beyond a home, money in the bank and thrifty living. Her husband's experience, his reading and his vision were way beyond her grasp, especially in the early years when he started teaching in a private college for a meagre salary.

Reading and discussions about politics and current events, which even her mother-in-law liked, were beyond her understanding. She kept silent when her fellow clerks in office discussed the news. She did not understand politics or approve of it. And her husband was not only a political scientist but someone steeped in the politics of the country. Soon, he went abroad, earned new degrees and a doctorate, and was appointed professor in a premier university in the capital, where he became part of a group of intellectuals who designed the academic future of the country. She was pleasantly surprised at this and enjoyed his popularity even if she did not fully appreciate his value.

As a family, they found a certain measure of happiness as the years went by. Though they had a couple of pretty daughters after their son's loss, the bitterness over their child's tragic and untimely death had scarred them both deeply. Jayanthi grew sharper and shrewder as she aged. She was suspicious, distrustful, withdrawn and often bitter. She carefully chose her friends from among people who were less qualified than her. She was insecure when the conversation turned to books, culture or politics. She preferred to discuss the rising prices of provisions, rare markets where things were sold cheap and the rising cost of living.

Music, books and cultural activities were beyond her grasp. She was a good working woman, housewife, a dutiful wife and mother. The one thing she was determined to ensure was that her daughters would never suffer any financial insecurity. She saved steadily, lived thriftily and ensured that her husband would not fritter her savings away. Though not an intellectual, she was extremely hard working, principled and efficient at her job. She rose steadily through promotions to the position of officer. Her daughters completed their studies and moved away to lead their own lives. They were efficient and hard-working women, just like their mother.

32

Being a man, Pankaja's eldest son, Seshadri, had plenty of exposure to the world. He also read widely, wrote extensively and gathered a considerable flock of admirers. Although popular, witty and charming in public, he was petty and irritable with his family and difficult to please. At home, he was often violent and brutal to his wife, perhaps resenting the fact that though educated, she could not fit into his circle of academic and political friends. She was a good mother, tending to her children's needs and saving for their future. She had to secure her family against her careless husband, who did not value wealth or think twice about wasting his money on books and donations.

He was often sarcastic and hurt her with his jokes, and while she respected him because he was successful and celebrated, she never quite grasped his true worth. Even while being in proximity with the circle of the intelligentsia in the capital, she never shed the mental attitude of the mofussil girl. Surrounded by scholarly, intelligent and politically-articulate women, he enjoyed his power and influence and made no attempt to draw her into his circle.

Ironically, this highly educated man could never overcome his deep resentment of his mother, Pankaja, for her independence and strength of will. He had countless political arguments with her about Rajaji and Gandhi. And he was always impressed by her sharpness. He never realised that if she had given in to his father, his own growth would have been warped and stunted by his unfaithful father's pettiness. It was his father's absence that had actually provided the space for him to struggle and grow. And yet, the unreasonable resentment towards his mother remained.

Pattamma, who was diabetic, also developed heart problems and took to her bed in her 50s. Once her hopes of having a grandchild died, she lost the will to survive. She died in her own bed, peacefully and with dignity, in her sister's arms. Rajappa performed her last rites with grace with his wife beside him. Life soon returned to normal and Pankaja, though grieving for her beloved sister, managed the house.

Some years later, Ramji who was the eternal Romeo, eloped with a girl who lived in a house down the street. She was a Tenaglia Brahmin and her father would never have agreed to the match though the Kandalas were Vadagalais, who were a notch superior in the Brahmin pecking order. After the couple eloped, the girl's father came with folded hands and bowed before Rajappa.

Weeping, he promised, 'I will perform the marriage. Just bring my daughter back. Let me show my face in public!'

Rajappa was moved and sent a team to trace the runaway couple. They were found after three days and Ramji was persuaded to return. The moment they came back, the father predictably locked up the girl and Ramji never saw her again. He stayed silent, mourning her loss for months. He neither ate anything nor spoke to anyone at home. Finally, Rajappa filed a writ of habeas corpus in the High Court. The girl was produced before the judge in his chambers.

She said, 'I have repented my wrongs and gone on a pilgrimage. I do not want to marry this man. I will obey my father.'

Rajappa was stunned at her statement and he suspected that Ramji would not survive the shock. But Ramji, strangely enough, heaved a sigh of relief and returned to his normal jovial self after that day.

The human heart is a mystery. Ramji's turnaround was inexplicable, but his family was thrilled about it. Pankaja promptly set about finding a bride for him. A girl called Seetha was chosen. She hailed from a once well-to-do and aristocratic family that had descended into poverty due to her father's gambling habit.

Ramji was a tall, fair and good-looking man. He had a decent job and came from a good family so his lack of a degree did not matter. Seetha was full of fun and her cheerful presence brought life into the house after the marriage. Husband and wife were happy with each other and they seldom disagreed on anything. Pankaja was finally at peace. She was delighted at Ramji's happiness.

About four years later, Rajappa who was now the secretary of the All-India Board of Cricket, had to leave for Pakistan as an issue had cropped up during the Indo-Pak series with the test team there. Travelling to Pakistan was not easy for him. He had pleaded with the judge for an adjournment of an ongoing case so he could travel, but the judge sternly refused. Crestfallen, he left the court wondering how to sort out the problem long distance. Cricket was his passion and he was desperate to see the series go on as scheduled. As he was getting into his car, the court clerk came running and said that his lordship had changed his mind and adjourned the case.

Rajappa rushed home, packed a bag and left for the airport. When he reached the departure lounge, the doors were already shut. He paused dejectedly. But an officer called the captain and said that his trip was of national importance. The aircraft doors were opened. Rajappa rushed into the aircraft in delight. He dozed off as the plane taxied down the runway and took off. After half-an-hour, he woke up, and sipping some coffee, began to make some notes on how to resolve the conflict. He was grateful to the judge for having changed his mind at the last minute. He would meet the good judge personally and thank him when he got back. Or better still, pick up a bottle of good Scotch at the duty-free section and gift it to him.

An hour passed quickly and the plane landed at Nagpur for refuelling. The passengers stood up and stretched their legs inside the aircraft. They were not allowed to disembark.

In about an hour, the flight was ready to take off again. It taxied down the runway and soared to the sky.

Pankaja was listening to the radio when she heard that the aircraft Rajappa had boarded had crashed at Nagpur. She froze in horror. Soon Ramji, his friends and a group of relatives crowded around her. There were no survivors. And it was time to decide who would go to claim his body.

Lakshmi said, 'Amma, let me go.'

Pankaja was shocked. She dismissed the idea, 'What is wrong with you, Lakshmi? Is it possible for you to visit that scene? Hush!'

She then turned to Comrade Iyengar, her sister's old friend, and said, 'His mother was fond of you. Do this last service for her child!'

Pankaja considered Pattamma a fortunate soul. After all, Pattamma had died a few years ago and escaped the ordeal of dealing with this unbearable sorrow. Pankaja's grief was deep. Rajappa had been so much more than a son to her, the precious child in a household of widows. The hope and dream of the clan. Her heart broke yet again quietly. His body was so charred that it was taken straight to the crematorium and the rites performed there. The women did not get to see his body. Pankaja's grief ate into her, deeply scarring her. Why had God forsaken her thus? Only a few days ago, she had been speaking of a friend who had lost her son, 'How could the mother deal with her grief?'

Well, fate had cruelly taught her a lesson within a few days of making that remark. She would never again ask such a question. Her cup was overflowing with sorrow. This deep, bitter grief would destroy her. How much sorrow can a woman stand before her heart is shattered beyond repair?

After the ceremony, Rajappa's wife Lakshmi returned to her father's house. All those years of humiliation that she suffered as an unwanted wife could not be erased by the fact that the rest of the family had respected her and loved her. She was bitter and left the disposal of Rajappa's assets and property, and his cases to her petty brother and father.

She resolved to avoid her dead husband's family and leave matters to her father and brother. Little did she know how misguided this decision was. Soon, the pettiness of her father and brother was on full display. They turned on her and harped on the fact that she was just a helpless widow.

'What did all this sense get you in your husband's house? You think because you are educated you can advise us? Go to your room and stay there, you wretched widow!'

Rajappa had never touched her but never once had he or anyone else in his family treated her with disrespect. When she retorted to them with contempt, they just stayed silent or politely refused to react to her remarks. They had tolerated her moods because they felt guilty about her husband's behaviour.

'All right, Lakshmi. Your wish, Amma! Whatever you say!' This was all they said to her no matter how rude she was.

No one outside the family had ever come to know that her husband had never touched her. It was a secret they would rather keep to themselves.

In the beginning, they used to ask her, 'Are you bathing every month?'

But soon, seeing her dull anger, they assumed that perhaps she was barren and withdrew the question. A cold fury raged inside her against, not only her husband but his whole family, though they had treated her with courtesy and respect. She felt they were responsible for her childless existence.

She had always prided herself on her education. It was only when her father and brother began to treat her with contempt after they had got hold of her assets that she realised how mistaken she was. She could have walked out of her in-laws' house years ago and gone to live in a hostel, studying or working, building an independent life for herself. But the advantages of being the wife of a prosperous lawyer had kept her from taking any risks. She had accepted her fate quietly.

A Telugu song from the film *Devdas* kept buzzing in her head:

Antha bhranthiyena? Jeevithana veluginthena?
Asha nirashena? Migiledhi chinteena?
(Is it all an illusion? Is this all the light in one's life?)
Is hope nothing but despair? Is it only sorrow that remains?)

Wisdom always dawns too late in life and she had no power to turn the clock back. Occasionally, one of Rajappa's cousins would visit her and for this courtesy, she was grateful.

33

As the years passed, Pankaja's life went on uneventfully. Occasionally, there would be news from Secunderabad about her husband. But time had blunted the pain of that loss and she was resigned to her life. She heard that Gopalan's children were restless and troublesome. Bhagya was bickering all the time with a man who was furious at being bedridden. She was not surprised. He had chosen his bed and must lie on it. She had no desire to turn into a ministering angel this late in life, bringing peace and comfort to a man who had hurt her so thoughtlessly. Outwardly calm, she listened to accounts of his suffering and worsening health. She hoped he would have understood at last how much effort it had taken for her to manage her life quietly all these years. To her, it seemed like he was learning the lesson that one paid for one's sins in this life as well as the next.

Janaki (Seetha), Pankaja's second daughter-in-law, was easy-going and carefree. Pankaja was happy to manage the house when she went to work. Janaki was not a home bird and did what she pleased, loafing around and having fun, regardless of her husband's disapproval. But they got along despite their differences. Theirs was a happy family by all accounts. Soon, Janaki conceived and delivered a baby girl.

Neither Jayanthi nor Janaki had brothers. Both came from a family of three sisters. Jayanthi's son was celebrated by her family before the irony and wilfulness of fate turned it into a tragedy. Janaki conceived again, nearly eight years after the birth of her daughter. This time, it was a son, and her family celebrated with great enthusiasm. And the child cried loudly and kicked sturdily when he was born. What good fortune it was to be the mother of a healthy son! Powerful feeling indeed!

He was cradled and named Gopala Krishna after both his grandfathers. Three weeks after the delivery, Janaki felt slightly feverish one evening. The doctor said it was nothing but the next morning, she was found unconscious in her bed. Her family rushed her to the hospital but it was too late. The doctors could not find a way to save her. She passed away before noon.

The baby boy lay in the cradle, smiling, blissfully

unaware of his mother's death, as the priest placed a straw in his hand and muttered a few *shlokas* and then handed it over to a cousin, who performed her last rites. Some relatives consoled Janaki's parents by saying that she was a fortunate woman to have borne a son to perform her last rites! A shattered Pankaja huddled in a corner, unable to believe that fate could be so cruel. How many more losses could she swallow? Pattamma, Rajappa, Ashok, and now this! Which God had trained his cruel gaze on her? What exactly was her sin? Who had she harmed?

She had tried to cope with every blow fate aimed at her by living her life simply. And yet, she was ruthlessly punished at every step. She had mourned Chellappa's child deeply, but she buried her grief before Jayanthi and her mother, lest, they thought she was being critical of them. She did blame the mother and daughter though. A home birth in a mofussil town for a woman in her late twenties? How could they have been so foolish and ignorant? And a disabled child walking several yards to an open well? Was that destiny? She felt guilty for all of it. Merely being a mother-in-law made her guilty! She wanted to scream and tear her hair out and shout at the sky. She wanted to beat her breast and bang her head against a pillar till she could quiet the thoughts troubling her.

In the end, she simply swallowed her grief and found the strength to carry on. This was but one more test for her. She did not wail loudly and just wiped her tears with her *pallu* quietly. Her calmness was wrongly interpreted by some people. They thought she was cold and unfeeling, but she had simply decided not to put her sadness on display. Putting on a brave front, she resumed her daily life.

She felt she was like Neelakanta, holding poison in her throat. Neither daring to swallow it lest it corrupt her life nor spit it out to poison those around her. But alas she was no Shiva, she had no Parvathi clasping her throat to hold the poison in place and not letting it slip. She was herself Ardhanarishwara, embodying both male and female principles in her indomitable will and all too frail flesh.

In Secunderabad, Gopalan's new family grew. His temper and his frustration increased by the hour as well. He was brutal to his children and disciplined them relentlessly. Bhagya could not manage even the normal mischief that her adolescent children indulged in and complained bitterly to their father. His only solution was to belt them. By the time they grew up,

Gopalan suffered heart trouble and he was crippled by arthritis as well.

He was too stubborn to admit even to himself that he had made a grave mistake by marrying a second time. If Pankaja had stayed, she would have restored some order in his life. Her presence would have given him the strength and will to discipline the children. He had foolishly underestimated her pride. He had always believed that she would relent her decision to leave one day and come back to him.

Once, when Ramji had written to him after school asking if he could send some extra money to cover his college fees, he replied scornfully that he had no intention of educating his first wife's children. They could pull rickshaws for a living for all he cared. Ramji had kept that postcard in his cupboard for many years. The message it conveyed was imprinted on his mind forever. Whether Gopalan was ever haunted by the message he sent to Ramji was anybody's guess.

Despite their father's neglect, Pankaja's children grew up to be fine, hard-working men, capable of making a decent living. Although Ramji was no scholar, he became a well-known trade unionist, respected by all his colleagues. Gopalan educated Bhagya's children well, as if to prove a point. The eldest, Raghuram, became a doctor, seduced and married a pretty cousin from

Bezawada, and left the country to set up his practice as a GP in Kent. He wanted to get as far away from his father as possible.

Although Gopalan had provided for his second wife's children well, they disliked and feared him intensely. Relieved that seven seas separated him from the father he abhorred, Raghuram settled down to a routine practice, content with the middle-class joys of a clean home, a dutiful wife and a nurse who was loyal to him and gladly provided him the occasional thrill of extra-marital sex.

After a few years, his dutiful wife surprised him by leaving him for a younger man who provided her with all the aspects of a good life that her husband knew nothing of. Eventually, with age, Raghuram grew weary, and his nerves weakened. He had trouble standing up and walking straight, and he returned to India, crippled and helpless. He breathed his last in Chennai. The young woman who tended to him during his last days cast his ashes into the Bay of Bengal as the bells of the Triplicane temple clanged loudly. His wife, who had left him several years ago for a cheerful younger man, did not waste any time grieving for him.

The second daughter, Lakshmi, also completed her medical degree. She was hastily married off to a second cousin of Bhagya's called Srinivasan. She agreed to the match because she was too scared of her father to marry one of her classmates. Besides she was afraid that as a second wife's daughter, she may not find a match at all and would have to stay single all her life. Srinivasan was much older than her and an eccentric. He gave her a miserable time. The only source of relief was her work. The minute she entered the hospital, she became another person: cool, calm and incredibly efficient. After the birth of her three children, she took off for a few years to work in the Gulf. Her mother-in-law, who made her life bearable, took care of the children while she was away.

When she came back to India, she had earned a tidy sum of money and was appointed chief of surgery at Apollo Hospital. Her husband whose liver had been damaged by excessive drinking, died in a couple of years, leaving her in peace.

She hardly went to see her father whom she detested though she kept in touch with her mother. Dark shadows clouded her life. Of her three children, her son died in a road accident. She accepted it with resignation because he was addicted to drugs and she had seen it coming. One daughter bore three girls and one fine day, leaving them with Lakshmi, she took off with a fellow she had picked up on the streets. Lakshmi had never been fond of motherhood, but she was forced to look after her grandchildren while waiting for her errant daughter to return.

Her son-in-law hung around for a couple of years and then took off. Once a year, a birthday card from her runaway daughter for one of the children would arrive from some remote place. By the time Lakshmi tried to trace her, she would be gone from that spot. Her third daughter married a man she loved but refused to have anything to do with Lakshmi. She never visited or spoke to her so she was as good as dead to Lakshmi. Bhagya, who had borne three children without earning their love or respect, was a comforting example to Lakshmi, who was forced to bear the weight of her children without feeling any of the affection or motherly love that could have lightened the load.

After winding up a brilliant professional life, desperate, worn out by the burdens of her truant children—one missing and another who would not speak to her—Lakshmi was deeply depressed. She knew that these were all punishments for her mother's crime. But why did she have to pay for her mother's stupidity? Why was she the one paying off the debt her mother had incurred? She was tormented by questions, but she did not expect solace from any source. It was ironic that Bhagya had no idea that her children detested her so much.

As a daughter, Lakshmi was torn between a sense of duty to her mother and her deep revulsion at her conduct. She knew that no one had any respect or affection for her mother. Bhagya was tolerated and she had visitors only because of her husband, whose patients and friends were loyal to him. She remembered with revulsion the large twin portraits of her parents that decorated their living room. It was as if the portraits were there to force visitors to believe that they were indeed a perfect couple. She shuddered at the memory.

One day, out of sheer boredom, Lakshmi went with a neighbour to a lecture by Sathya Sai Baba. This became a turning point in her life. Her world was transformed and she was transported to a totally different state of mind thanks to the lecture. Like the hundreds of people around her, she found immense solace in his gentle voice. A voice that caressed her and comforted her as it seeped into every pore, dissolving her sorrows. All her grief and frustration melted away. Closing her eyes, she chanted his *bhajans* fervently. She pressed the imprint of his feet to her head and heart. She could feel her heart beat quicken as her skin prickled with joy. Suddenly, life had acquired new meaning.

After all her suffering, God had opened his eyes, and her reward was this bliss that washed over her being. Every word uttered in Baba's gentle voice sent shivers of joy down her spine. Her suffering was a thing of the past. At last, at long last, she was fulfilled and safe. She did not worry about her grandchildren either. Baba would take care of all. Baba, the lord of miracles. She had seen him performing miracles, producing sacred ash out of thin air.

She held a white silver coin with his image engraved on it to her heart. Her granddaughter pointed out that it had 'made in China' printed on the back. But she refused to see or hear anything. He was her saviour. Her God. The reward for all the years of suffering and loneliness she had endured. She was enclosed in the warmth of his love and safe from all harm in the cocoon of his care.

Gopalan's third son, Ranganath (Rangu), was the brightest of all his children. He joined medical college, found it a crashing bore and enlisted in the Indian Air Force instead. Gopalan, with great foresight, said that if his son died in an air crash, he could at least weep for him. But if he came back alive, he would have to mourn the fact that he was still alive.

During his travels, Rangu met Molly, an attractive young scientist from Manipur. She was a fair, slim woman with chiselled features The two fell in love, got married and lived happily together briefly. They also had a lovely daughter. But old habits die hard. Rangu was a hard drinker and a creature of moods. Weary of dealing with his addictions and mood swings, Molly left him one day, taking her daughter with her.

A brilliant pilot, Rangu was admired and loved by his colleagues and his squadron leader. He was born to fly. But he began to down several pegs before he boarded a flight. Though he was the best pilot around, his commanding officer soon realised that he was a flight risk and grounded him. The Indo-Pak war was going on and though his skill would have been critical at the time, his drinking made him a liability. He was grounded and put in charge of the control tower. The country was at war and his expertise was crucial.

But, as he guided planes across the skies from his post at the tower, he began to miss the thrill of flying. He yearned for the adrenaline surge he would feel as he soared to the sky and came diving down to hit a target. The power and glory that coursed through his veins as he flew through enemy territory could not be matched by manning a control tower, however crucial the job may be. The skies beckoned him. The call was irresistible.

One day, requesting his colleague to manage the tower and assuring him he would be back soon, Rangu walked out. It was hours before his colleague realised he was gone for good. A red alert was sent out for him. By then, he had hopped on a lorry, travelled south and was hundreds of miles away. Hopping on trains and lorries, he made his way home. His father was shocked and his mother, hysterical. Covered with dust, his hair caked with dirt, and his beard overgrown, he looked like a stranger.

He collapsed in front of his alarmed parents. His mother called for help to pick him up and move him into a bed. After he was washed and shaved, he looked a pitiful skeleton, a shadow of the handsome man in uniform. Of all their children, he looked most like his father. Once a tall, good-looking man, now a pitiful and gaunt figure. His liver and pancreas were badly damaged.

Gopalan muttered, 'I said that if he died in a crash I could weep for his loss. Now, I have to weep that he is still alive.'

God in his infinite wisdom had opened his eyes and brought Rangu back so that his father could grieve that he was alive. Whether, in the course of this suffering Gopalan ever thought this was his punishment for what he had done to Pankaja, no one could tell. He often told people that there was no hell after life. Hell was right here…

Rangu was traced in no time by the military police. Desertion and dereliction of duty, especially at war time, held serious consequences. Given his brilliant record and the fact that he had a squadron leader for a godfather saved him from the misery of a military prison. He was declared mentally ill and released on grounds of mercy. He hung about his parents' house, gaunt and diseased, the ghost of the most brilliant of Bhagya's children.

Out of the blue, some years later, Molly sent him a picture of his grown daughter. Rangu gazed at it for a long time. Grief, regret and shame washed over him. He spent hours in front of the picture. That night, he found a thick rope and slinging it through the iron loop in the ceiling, made a noose. Pulling a chair close, he climbed on it, slipped the noose round his neck and kicked the chair away. Bhagya found him the next morning. Shocked and distraught, she screamed for help. The neighbours cut him down and he miraculously went on to make a recovery. He still had one duty left to perform.

He survived for a few more years, long enough to provide the fourth shoulder to bear his father's body. That duty done, he wasted away and died. His passing was a release. Though he was her favourite child, even Bhagya did not mourn his loss.

Gopalan had grown steadily worse. He could barely move or breathe. His heart was beyond help. Pankaja's sons turned up to see him and his eyes scanned the room for her. But Pankaja had refused to come. She would not give him the satisfaction of seeing her under the same roof as Bhagya. She could not stomach deathbed scenes, where he might try to unite his two wives to satisfy his ego. Or worse, entrust Bhagya to her care. Gopalan sighed a bitter sigh, and turning his face to the wall, gave up. Death was inevitable. Pankaja's coming could not halt that. But could she not submit to his dearest wish to see both his wives under the same roof during the last moments of his life?

The answer was a firm no. Pankaja would not give in, not after she had struggled all these years to keep her pride and dignity intact. Even her children felt that she could try to oblige a dying a man. But they would never understand how revolting it was for her to bow her head and step into a house that had betrayed her and crushed her dreams mercilessly. She no longer cared if people thought she was hard hearted. This man had fathered her children and then destroyed all her chances of happiness while he went chasing a mirage. It was time for him to feel that same loss of hope, that sense of betrayal and sting of cruelty. It was his fate to scan an empty space for a final goodbye.

She was calm and unemotional. After all that she had lived through and endured, his death was an anti-climax. Except for the fact that it would deny her the dream of a smear of turmeric and the garland of fresh flowers that decked a *sumangali*'s body. Well, so be it. She came from a house of widows after all...

Gopalan's funeral was a sorry affair. His four sons were there to carry his body to the ghat. But the grandeur and the outpouring of grief he had imagined would follow because of his fame and popularity as a doctor was missing. Bhagya thought bitterly about how he had imagined he would have a grand funeral with a huge crowd of patients grieving the loss of their beloved doctor. A stampede was what he would have liked. But he had been sick and out of sight too long. Except for a clutch of tenants and neighbours, there was no one at the funeral. He was forgotten, irrelevant. There was no grief at all. Just an impatience to get it over with.

Only his sons looked upset. The shoulders that bore his body had in different ways borne the brunt of his rage and ego. All of them were lost in thought.

The eldest, carrying the pot of embers, was the most collected of the lot. He had been far stronger than his father.

The funeral ceremonies were conducted by his sons in Koneru, an auspicious hall with a pond reserved for such events. Pankaja remained in Chellappa's house. On the tenth day, she broke her *taali* string and unscrewed the diamond nose pin that had never left her nose for fifty years. She poured water over her head, washing off all memories of the man, who had ruthlessly destroyed her life. Leaving the jewels in the puja corner, she beat her breast a couple of times symbolically. And she emerged bright and beautiful. As always.

Later, she had the diamonds set in rings for her sons who had performed the ceremonies. Being symbols of widowhood, they could not be gifted to her daughters or daughters-in-law. Amused, she thought of the proverb, 'far better a clean-shaven, shining head than a disgusting husband!'

The widowhood she had dreaded like a nightmare since her childhood was just a bubble. A myth. The worst was over. She was finally at peace. In a few weeks, she returned to Madras, untarnished. She glowed, pure and bright, unencumbered by the miseries of widowhood. It was as if a rock had been lifted off her back.

She was free at last.

She was Pankaja.

Bhagya, on the other hand, suffered for her sins. Her children were small comfort. Her sons had not cared for her. The younger one, after his attempt at suicide, died of a diseased pancreas. She was not without means though. She was comfortable with her pension and the money her husband had provided, but lacked all human warmth. Her brothers were dead. Her sons detested her. Her daughter was cold towards her. Though she had been a good teacher, she had no group of loyal students who admired her or visited her.

She lived a pathetic, lonely life in the house Gopalan had built for her until she took ill. When she collapsed on the doorstep one day, a neighbour admitted her in a geriatric home where she continued to breathe and vegetate for several years. All the money she had saved so carefully through the years went into her care. Her son and daughter did not bother to visit her. It was a life wasted, waiting for release. When she died her body was handled by the home authorities. No child or kin to place that last handful of rice on her mouth, or sprinkle water on her cold body. Twice widowed, she was not entitled to flowers anyway.

All she had wanted in life was some measure of happiness. And she had reached out greedily to grasp another's happiness as if it was a ripe fruit dangling from a tree, ready for the picking.

Bhagya had never grasped the bitter truth that Pankaja's happiness was pure hard work; built brick by brick, cemented firmly by strength, sacrifice and self-denial. That, in the long run, married bliss was a myth. A bubble that burst if touched.

Epilogue

Jagan walked out of the hall. As his friends congratulated him and thumped his shoulders, his eyes darted around, searching the grounds eagerly for Jalaja. This was graduation day at JIPMER. Jagan had topped the list of medical students. He was very happy. He could now specialise in thoracic surgery, which fascinated him. At last, his mother would be content. She had suffered deeply while bringing him up and he had resolved never to give her a moment's anxiety. His father, however, was far more detached. A step-father after all!

Suddenly, he heard a cheerful voice and felt a gentle touch on his shoulder. Jalaja had topped the list in biochemistry. Holding up their gold medals, they looked at each other and burst into peals of delighted laughter. Jalaja hugged him and held him close for a minute. Their friends laughed loudly and cheered.

'Two gold medals clanging will catch fire, be careful!'

Amidst all the noise and cheering and laughter Jalaja clung tightly to Jagan's hand. She was breathless with joy. They answered all their friends' questions, promised to meet them for dinner to celebrate, and slipped away quietly.

They headed to the beach so that they could be spend some time together at a quiet place. They had first met at a seminar and had earnest discussions over coffee. Jalaja felt she was meant to be with Jagan from the moment they met. They grew close and realised that they were in love, but had to keep a careful distance from each other. They were well-aware of the amount of damage that a single envious professor or intolerant assistant could wreak. Brilliance in students who did not bow down before their professors was not tolerated. They worked hard, barely speaking to each other in public and meeting secretly outside the campus.

Jalaja was acutely aware of how difficult it was for a student like Jagan, who happened to be a Dalit, to overcome caste resentment even in an excellent campus like theirs. But his academic brilliance, hard work and modesty saw him through. He was never arrogant or complacent about his success.

Jagan's mother was the principal of one of the oldest schools in Nellore. A couple of her uncles had studied there many years ago. Jalaja's father Ramji had retired as an officer from Life Insurance Corporation and her mother Lakshmi was a retired banker. An only child, they had cherished and pampered her, naming her Jalaja in accordance with family tradition. All Rajamma's granddaughters were named after the lotus flower according to her wish. Lakshmi had married Ramji after he lost his first wife, Janaki, due to complications from childbirth. Jalaja dearly loved her half-brother and half-sister, Srilekha and Krishna. She enjoyed the warmth of their company and their humour during their annual visits to Madras. They lived in Singapore and Germany and visited India only once a year.

Jalaja's parents knew she was interested in a young man at her Institute. They were eager to meet him. Since they trusted Jalaja's judgement completely, they were willing to wait till she was certain. All they wanted was for her to be happy. She was a bright girl and her parents did not feel any anxiety about her life choices.

Jagan's mother, however, was not at all happy. She was extremely nervous and ill at ease. This was certainly not the family she wanted her son to marry into. She wished he would take some more time to make up his mind. She herself had paid dearly for her haste. He was puzzled that in spite of knowing all the necessary details about Jalaja's family, his mother was so doubtful. Her hesitation was due to the fact that her son was precious to her and she wanted his progress to continue unhindered. She did trust Jagan, but she was in doubt about this particular choice of his. This girl? This family? Of all the girls he must have met, was this the only one he was drawn to!

Though uneasy, she stayed quiet in order to keep the peace. She had never told Jagan how or why his father died. She had lied to him that his father had suffered a fatal accident. And in a way it was! One of those accidents that fate plays on mortals...

One evening, when a cool sea breeze was wafting across the verandah, the doorbell rang. Lakshmi set aside the newspaper she was reading and went to open the door. Her husband was engrossed in watching a cricket match on TV. He turned around when he heard her cry of delight.

Jalaja, back from Pondicherry, was the picture of happiness. Behind her stood a quiet young man. He was dark, tall and lithe. After they had been introduced to each other and coffee and bondas were served, they began to chat. Jalaja's parents touched both the gold medals with awe and were filled with delight. The conversation then moved on to family and the future. Jalaja's mother asked Jagan, 'So, it seems you come from Nellore? Our family is also from there.'

'Yes, my mother told me,' Jagan said. 'Her name is Krupa. She retired from PS High School.'

There was a brief silence. An uneasy stillness.

'And your father?' asked Lakshmi.

'He died when I was a child. A tragic accident snatched him away from us. I am named after him.'

Jalaja's father choked on his coffee. Her mother turned pale as a ghost.

'You do realise I am Mala by caste, I hope?' Jagan looked at them questioningly.

Jalaja scoffed. 'Jagan, please! They are not so backward. My sister divorced her husband and married a Parsi colleague of hers from Singapore.'

Ramji gasped as he rose from his chair and lurched sideways. Vivid memories of his cousin Jagan came rushing back: Jagan's life, his death, and the last call from him, which Ramji had not answered. There were many regrets to grapple with.

'Jagannathan, forgive us our sins. You are the lord of mercy! The saviour of the world!' Ramji murmured, crashing on the floor.

His head swam as the room suddenly grew pitch dark. He had a vision of a huge cobra raising its shining hood as it swayed, its forked tongue darting in and out. He was frozen from shock. The sight made his heart pound and his breath caught in his throat. The past had come full circle. The curse of the Kandalas. The *sarpa dosha*! Jagannathan's face hovered over him grimly. Gasping for air, he passed out.

The ambulance wound its way down the crowded streets to the hospital. The sun was setting. The sea was ominously calm. Lakshmi murmured a prayer to Jagannathan who smiled: a stony god, calm and distant, completely untouched by human misery.

Acknowledgements

I am as ever indebted to Srinidhi, whose patience and unwavering faith in my ability helped me to finish this tale.